STO

FRIENDS
OF ACPL

P9-BZL-533

Sea View Secret

SEA VIEW

SECRET

BY ELIZABETH KINSEY

ILLUSTRATED BY MARY STEVENS

JC629s

FRANKLIN WATTS, *Incorporated*

699 MADISON AVENUE, NEW YORK 21, N. Y.

Copyright 1952 by FRANKLIN WATTS, INC.

First Printing

Designed by Leonard W. Blizard

Manufactured in the United States of America by the Country Life Press

Contents

Sea View Secret

CHAPTER 1

A Brand-New House

This is the story of what happened to Peter and Jane Bowman the summer they moved to Sea View Gardens.

Peter was eleven. He was big for his age. When he wasn't in school, or out playing ball, he liked to make ship models. He was also very good about helping in the house or doing errands.

That was lucky for his mother, who was a writer. Besides Peter and Jane there were two babies in the family. Mother wouldn't have had much time for writing if it had not been for Peter and Jane.

The Bowman family lived in the city on the top floor of an old apartment house, and there was no elevator. Ever since the twins were born there had been a great deal of work to do in the Bowman household. Every time Mother had to take the twins to the park it was an awful job. She would carry one twin and Jane would take the other and Peter would carry all the blankets and pillows. They would go downstairs and get them all stowed in the carriage and then Mother would remember a bottle or a rattle or her book, and Peter or Jane would have to go back for it.

And the amount of washing that had to be done for those two babies! Peter couldn't understand the number of shirts and nightgowns and diapers that babies wore. It seemed like hundreds. Every day he and Jane had to help hang out all those clothes.

So by the time the twins were ten months old, Mother and Dad decided that the only thing to do was to get a house in a suburb so that the twins could be put out in the back yard, and Mother could get her writing done. And when that happened, the first thing Peter and Jane would be able to have would be a dog (if you can call a dog a thing) and the next would be bicycles, which they had never been able to have in the city.

Jane was ten. She wore her black hair short, with bangs, so that she didn't always need to be combing it, and she wore dungarees when she wasn't in school. Peter wore his hair in a crew cut, so he *never* had to comb it, and he wore dungarees all the time.

10

Mother would carry one twin and Jane the other

Jane was going to be a famous woman writer when she grew up. In the meantime she was busy reading all the books in the public library. She especially liked mystery stories and books about old houses where some priceless treasure had been buried for centuries. She said she was reading them to learn how to write, but Peter said that was just an excuse to read all the time.

Peter liked reading too, but he didn't care to spend all his time at it. He was more interested in making things. His favorite subject in school was shop, and his father helped him with his model-building at home.

Peter was interested in ships because his father was a ship's engineer. Peter was very proud of this. He had a large picture of his father's ship, the *Mary K. Sterling*, on the wall of his room, and he knew it so well that he could have drawn it from memory. It had two funnels, each with two blue stripes and one red stripe.

The only drawback to having a father who was a ship's engineer was that Dad had to keep going off on voyages. Peter hoped that some day he would be able to go with his father. In the meantime he made ship models.

One Saturday, about the middle of June, when Dad had been ashore (on the beach, he called it) for several weeks, and had spent most of that time looking for a house, he announced that he had found one that he thought would do. It was in a place outside the city called Sea View Gardens.

"Hooray!" said Peter. "Can you see the sea from there?"

"No," said Dad. "It's ten miles from the sea. I don't know why it's called Sea View Gardens."

"But it must mean something," said Peter.

"Well, I don't know," said Dad. "Maybe if you could climb up onto the top of a very tall tree you might get a glimpse of the sea, only there aren't any very tall trees near our house. I guess it's just a name for a real-estate development."

Jane got all excited. "Oh, goody!" she exclaimed, and she jumped up and down the way she always did when she was excited about something, her black hair bouncing with each jump. "I hope we're going to move to a big old mysterious house with secret stairways."

"No, we're not," said Dad. "We will move to a brand-new small modern bungalow with no stairs at all."

Jane stopped jumping.

"Oh!" she said. "But old mysterious houses are so nice."

"Oh, yes," said Dad. "But so are small modern ones. They're nice for Mother because there isn't so much work to do in them."

Well, Jane understood that all right. "When can we go there?" she asked.

"We can go today and look at it," said Dad. "How about right now?"

Mother was just as eager as the children to see it, so she quickly packed a lunch and a couple of suitcases full of extra diapers and bottles for the twins, and they all went down and got into the car, and Peter only had to run up again twice more for things that Mother had forgotten before they were really on their way.

Jane asked a few more times whether Father was sure there weren't any secret staircases, and when he said there weren't, she finally kept still and just looked out of the window.

The twins fell asleep in the back seat and all was peaceful.

They passed through the city and over a bridge and then through lots of suburbs. First there were just a lot of ugly gas stations. Then there were houses with shady trees and big yards. Then they came to lots of newer and smaller houses, all alike, rows and rows of them, looking like toy villages cut out of cardboard.

Dad said, "We're getting close."

They drove on a bit farther, past a railroad station and some stores, and then Dad stopped the car in front of a real-estate office. A small green car was parked in front of it.

"I'll just go in and get the agent to take us to the house," he said. He got out of the car and pretty soon he came back with a stout, red-faced man.

"This is Mr. Krautkopf," he said.

"Oh, so this is the family," said the man. "Such lovely children. Are you coming to live out here in one of our houses?" And he reached into the car and patted Peter on the head, and then he pinched Jane's cheek. Peter didn't like to be patted on the head, and Jane liked even less to have her cheek pinched.

"We've come to look at the house," Mother said.

The man got into the small green car and started

off, and Dad followed him. They drove about a mile, past rows of little houses, and finally they stopped in front of one of them. It was just like all the others. Father stopped his car too.

"How does he know which it is?" Jane whispered to Peter.

"I guess he can tell because it's got no curtains in the windows," said Peter.

They all got out and went up the walk, leaving the twins asleep in the car. Mr. Krautkopf unlocked the door and they went in.

Mother and Dad went around examining everything—the floors, the walls, the faucets in the kitchen, and the furnace, which was in a little room next to the kitchen.

The house really had no stairs, just as Dad had said. It was all on one floor, which would be good, Peter thought, in case anybody forgot anything.

Mother loved it, and she had to go back and examine everything again and again. The kitchen was what she loved most. It had a big new refrigerator and a washing machine and a wonderful electric stove and a beautiful sink, and most wonderful of all, a dish-washing machine!

Jane and Peter, however, had soon seen everything there was to see in the house.

"Come on out," said Peter. "Let's see what there is outside."

They went out and looked around. It was hot. There was no shade anywhere around the house. There was a small lawn in front and a small yard in back, and a white picket fence around the whole thing, and there was a very small tree planted in the middle of the lawn, but it was too young and skinny to give any shade.

Peter and Jane looked at the houses across the street. They were just the same.

"I wonder where the kids play here," said Peter.

"In the street, I guess," said Jane. They looked up and down the street but they couldn't see any children. In one yard there was a baby in a play pen, and there were baby carriages in front of some of the houses, but no sign of any children their age.

And it didn't look like a very good street for playing. It was so hot and sunny and dusty.

"Maybe there's a park," said Peter. He went out into the middle of the road and looked around, and sure enough, way down at the end of the street there was a big patch of green trees. He could see them waving above the roofs of the little houses.

Just then Mother and Dad and Mr. Krautkopf came out, all talking at once, and Mr. Krautkopf smiled at Peter and tried to pinch Jane's cheek again, but she dodged. Peter tried to ask about the green trees, but the grownups were too busy discussing mortgages and taxes and plumbing to pay any attention.

Jane yanked Mother's sleeve and said, "We're going for a walk."

Mother nodded absent-mindedly and off they went.

They walked along the sidewalk and looked at the little houses as they went past. Nearly every one had some sort of baby gear out in front. There were a couple of tiny tricycles and a very small doll carriage that looked as though they might belong to three-year-olds. And it was getting hotter, too.

"It'll be nice in the park," said Peter.

At last they got there. There was an iron fence all along the sidewalk, and inside were lots of great tall trees and thick bushes and tall grass. It looked rather neglected, but it seemed shady and cool inside.

"I wonder how you get in," said Jane. But there was no entrance to be seen. They went around a corner and there was a gate but it was locked.

"This is a funny park," said Peter.

But Jane had been peering between the bushes and suddenly she let out a whoop.

"It's not a park," she said. "There's a house in there, a big old mysterious house!"

Peter peered too. Sure enough, there was a tall house. A driveway led to the gate, but it was overgrown with weeds as if it hadn't been used in years.

They walked around to the side of the house. Here the bushes were thinner and they got a better view. The house had three stories and there was a little square box stuck on the top, like a lookout tower, with windows on the two sides that they could see.

"Oh, boy!" said Jane. "I bet that house has secret stairways and sliding panels and everything."

"Well, maybe," said Peter, "but what interests

me more is that yard. You could have a good game of cops and robbers among those bushes. I wonder who lives there."

They stared as hard as they could, but there was no sign of life.

"I guess it's shut up," said Jane.

"Well, come on back," said Peter. "We'll ask that man about it."

They ran back along the street to their house. The only way they knew it was that the two cars were parked in front of it.

The twins had awakened, and Mother was sitting in the back of the car feeding them water out of bottles. Father and Mr. Krautkopf were walking around looking at the outside of the house. Mr. Krautkopf was even redder than before, with the heat, and was fanning himself with his hat.

Jane burst on him like a thunderbolt. "What's that big house way over there with the trees around it?" she demanded.

The man scowled, but then he smiled sweetly and said, "Oh, that! That's the house we couldn't get. But we'll get it yet."

Dad looked interested. "Why do you want it?" he asked.

Mr. Krautkopf didn't answer directly. "Oh, well," he said, "we bought up all the places around here. There were lots of big houses like that one."

"What happened to them?" Peter asked.

"Oh, we tore 'em down," replied Mr. Krautkopf. "Had to, to make room for all these bungalows. But the old lady who lives in that one wouldn't sell. She's peculiar."

"What do you mean?" Dad asked.

"Slams the door in your face. Won't let anybody come near. You kids better stay away from there."

Peter was sorry to hear that. But Jane looked as if she didn't believe him.

"I bet there's something mysterious about that house," she said hopefully.

Peter didn't put so much stock in that—he just wished he could get to play in that big garden. But after all, you needed kids to play with, not just a cross old lady.

Mother and Dad, however, were all excited about the little house they had come to see. Dad said it was a good buy, and just what he could afford, and that when they got an awning put up, and some trees and flowers planted, it wouldn't look so bare.

Peter thought it looked a bit dull, but of course he could see that it would be much better for them all to be here than on the top floor of an old city apartment house.

So when Mother and Dad asked if Peter and Jane liked the place, they said yes.

"The only thing wrong is that it isn't a bit mysterious," Jane complained. "Nothing exciting could happen in it. You'd never discover a treasure in it, for instance."

"Don't be too sure," said Father.

CHAPTER 2

Sailing Orders

The next two weeks were so full of activity that Peter and Jane didn't know whether they were coming or going. Of course they were going, but they couldn't just get up and go. First all their belongings had to be packed, and that was quite a job because the babies had to be taken care of all the time just the same.

The twins had learned to crawl by the time they were ten months old, and they were underfoot all the time, picking up pieces of paper and dust and thumb tacks and trying to eat everything they picked up.

"Belay that!" Peter kept shouting at them, but they didn't pay any attention.

So he put them in the brig, which was the nautical term he used for the play pen, and that made them howl. Then he suggested lending them to some friends till the moving was finished, but Mother wouldn't hear of it, so they just had to keep a weather eye out for them and make the best of it.

By the first of July they were installed in their new house, but that didn't mean they could sit down and take things easy. Everything had to be unpacked again, chairs and tables set in place, dishes and books put on shelves.

In the morning, when there was some shade in the back yard, because the sun was in front of the house, the twins were put out there on the grass. In the afternoon the shade was in front, and they were put there. In the middle of the day there was no shade, so they had to be kept in the house.

Dad had about two more weeks before he had to go on board ship. He helped Peter fix up his room. It was a good big room, with plenty of space for a work bench, and over the work bench were two shelves to display his ship models. Peter had decided to display only the best ones. There was a schooner, a battleship, a tanker, a model of Father's ship with the red-and-blue stripes on its funnels, and now Peter was working on something really hard—a full-rigged sailing ship. He would have liked to have Dad help him with it, but there wasn't time.

There was all the rest of the house to do. Mother's study had to be made ready for her to work in. Dad gave her desk a coat of paint and helped her arrange her files and bookshelves.

Then he got busy in the garden and planted bushes next to the house. He put a trellis on one wall and planted some vines that would grow quickly. He put up an awning and planted geraniums under the front windows, and soon it really started to look like home.

Of course Peter and Jane wanted to be with him as much as possible, so they didn't bother about exploring the neighborhood.

Dad was playing the game he always played before he went off. He pretended that the house was a ship, and that she was being made ready for a long voyage. Mother was the Captain, Peter was the First Mate, Jane was Second Mate. Once Jane had been called Able Seaman, but she claimed that that meant she had too much work to do, especially washing dishes in the galley (which was what they called the kitchen), so from that time on she and Peter were both called Mates. The twins were Midshipmen because they had so much to learn.

Dad made the two Mates scrape barnacles and

chip rust (which were his names for sweeping and scrubbing), and every time they went to the grocery he called it the ship's chandler and said they were laying in stores for a long voyage around the Horn.

This was fun, of course, but at last the time came when he had to leave (only he pretended that *they* were leaving). It was his last day ashore. His bags were packed and he had to leave before supper.

He asked Peter and Jane if they wanted to go for a walk. They didn't really want to, but they started out anyhow and walked slowly down the street.

"Maybe we can find a place where they sell ice-cream sodas," Dad said. And as they walked along he told them he was counting on them to help the Captain and see that the Midshipmen didn't bilge, which meant get into trouble.

He always gave them this kind of talk before leaving, to buck them up. Then just before sailing time he usually handed them a couple of envelopes which he said were their orders, and not to be opened until he was gone. The orders were a surprise, and were usually something pretty good.

The last time, Peter's orders consisted of plans for a new ship model—the two-masted schooner which was now on display over his work bench, and the

27

first sailing ship he had made. He had been so busy making her that he had hardly noticed how long Dad was gone.

Jane's orders had been a blank book and a ball-point pen with which she was supposed to write stories. That was when she got so interested in mysterious houses. She had started a novel called *The Mystery of the Ruined Castle,* only she never finished it because she got too interested in reading the books in the library.

They were wondering what their orders would be this time. But Dad wouldn't give them a hint. They ate their ice cream in the drugstore, and then they came out and looked in the window of the hardware store next door, because Dad wanted to buy some garden tools. There in the window was a box with some puppies in it. They were black spaniel pups about three months old. They were fat and lively, and very cute. They were wrestling and biting each other with their little teeth. Every few minutes one would stop and sit up and look around, and the others would jump on him and start wrestling all over again.

Peter and Jane didn't want to stop looking at them, so Dad went inside and bought a hoe and a

They were fat and lively little puppies

rake and a garden hose and told the man to send them at five o'clock.

Then he came out and they went home again and passed the time somehow. This was the time Peter hated worst. It was very hard to think of anything to say or do when somebody was just leaving and everything had already been done. They all sat around, and once in a while Mother or Dad would say, "Well, take care of everything," or "Don't forget to write."

Peter would have liked to go to his room and work on his ship model, except that it wouldn't have been polite.

Fortunately the twins decided to eat the ashes out of the ash trays, and everybody had to jump up and stop them, which gave them all something to do.

Then at last it was half-past four, and Mother went out to get the car from the garage.

Dad kissed Jane and shook hands with Peter and handed him an envelope.

"Orders, Mister Mate," he said, saluting. "For you and Second Mate. Good luck!" Then he left.

They watched through the window and saw him get into the car. He waved, and Mother drove off.

"Open it," said Jane, gloomily. Peter could tell

she was disappointed not to have an envelope of her own. He tore it open and took out a sheet of paper which read:

```
Stand by for active duty.

Instructions will be forwarded to you.

                    The Commander.
```

They stared at each other. They didn't know what to make of this. Never before had Dad left any such orders as these.

They sat down to mind the twins, feeling very low in spirit and wishing their father didn't have a job that took him far away while other fathers just went to the city and came home every night.

But just as they were really beginning to feel sorry for themselves, the doorbell rang.

Jane went to answer it, and Peter heard her give a startled "Oh!"

He got up and rushed to her aid, calling out, "All hands on deck!"

There on the front doorstep was the man from the hardware store. He had just driven over in his truck. His arms were full. He had the hoe and the rake

and the hose in one arm, and in the other was a cardboard box.

"Mr. Peter Bowman and Miss Jane Bowman?" he asked.

"That's us," Peter said.

"Well, these things are for you," he said. He stood the tools against the wall and set the box down. On the top were the words: "Orders. Break seal at once."

"What is it?" Peter asked.

The man grinned. "Your orders," he said. "But watch those two characters." And he pointed to the twins, who had crawled over and were trying to take a bite out of the hose. Peter rescued the hose and pulled the top off the box.

Out jumped a black puppy!

It was so happy to get out of the box that it leaped and pranced about, and jumped at the twins and licked their faces, and bounced at Peter and Jane. They were so surprised that they sat down on the floor and tried to catch it, and just kept saying, "Oh, golly! Oh, my!"

The man from the hardware store just stood there and grinned.

Finally the puppy got tired and sat down, with its paws spread apart foolishly and its red tongue hanging out.

"Well," said Jane, "that's the best orders we've had yet. What shall we call him?"

Peter thought about that for a moment.

"I know," he said. "We've got captains and mates and midshipmen, but we haven't any lieutenant. Why don't we call him the Lieutenant?"

"Okay," said Jane. "I mean aye, aye, sir." And

she saluted.

The puppy sat up and rubbed his nose with his paw. It looked just as if he were saluting too. Jane grabbed him and gave him a hug.

The hardware-store man laughed. "Well, so long, kids," he said. "I guess the Lieutenant will have a good berth with you. I'll report to his former owner."

"Okay," said Peter. "You can tell whoever it is that we'll take good care of him."

CHAPTER 3

The Lieutenant Runs Away

U. S. 5798676

Well, the Lieutenant was a welcome addition to the family. Mother wasn't surprised—it seemed she knew about it all the time—and she liked him just as much as Peter and Jane did. It was true it made three babies to take care of instead of two, but that was all right.

The very next morning Peter and Jane got busy on the other part of their orders, which included using the rake and hoe and the garden hose. They took the twins and the puppy out in the back yard and let them romp on the grass. The twins kept trying to catch the Lieutenant, but they couldn't. He was too quick for them. Still it kept them busy while Peter and Jane dug the flower beds, and while they were all busy in the garden, Mother got under way with her new book. Peter and Jane had made an agreement with her. They would mind the twins for

35

two hours every morning so that she could write her book, and when it was done they would both get bicycles. They certainly hadn't expected to get the puppy so soon.

Never had two hours gone so fast. The first thing they knew it was half-past eleven, and Mother put her head out of the study window and called, "All right, bring them in. They can crawl around in here while I get lunch."

They lugged the babies inside and ran out again.

"Let's take a walk," Peter said. "We've got an hour before the kids are fed and put to bed."

"Okay," said Jane, "and let's keep a sharp lookout for somebody our age."

They called the Lieutenant and started off down the street. He waddled along after them—they had no leash for him—stopping every now and then to growl at a pebble or worry a piece of grass. But pretty soon he sat down and cried.

"He's tired," said Jane.

"You're right," said Peter. "And besides, the sidewalk's too hot for his feet." Peter could feel the heat of the pavement burning through his own shoes. The sky was bright blue, and the mid-July sun shone down hotter every minute.

Peter picked up the puppy, who snuggled down in his arms and closed his eyes. They walked along, looking to right and left, but not a child did they see.

Pretty soon they met a lady pushing a baby carriage with one hand and pulling a child on a tricycle with the other. She was Mrs. MacDermott, their next-door neighbor.

"Hello," she said. "I see you've got a new member in your family." She tickled the Lieutenant behind the ears and he woke up and licked her hand. "Now you'll have someone to play with."

Jane said, "We were hoping we'd find some children our age around here."

Mrs. MacDermott shook her head. "I don't think there are any," she said. "I think they're all little. Teddy is three, and he's one of the big ones." She meant the little boy on the tricycle. "We've just been to play with Teddy's friend Oscar, and now we must hurry home to lunch." Her baby had started to cry, and she went on hurriedly, "Do come and see me."

Peter and Jane said they would, and walked on. Peter was beginning to get worried. He and Jane got along very well, but after all, they did need someone else to play with once in a while. But he

Suddenly the Lieutenant escaped through the fence

didn't say anything because just then they came in sight of the big house and the green trees. They hurried to walk in the shade of the trees that hung over the fence. It was a relief to get out of the sun.

Peter put the Lieutenant down. He sniffed at the fence, and then suddenly he gave a happy bark and jumped right through.

"Come back!" Peter shouted to him. "Here, Lieutenant! Come back here!"

But the puppy paid no attention. He just ran around on the grass. Soon he sat down and looked at the children. Then he got up and trotted out of sight.

Jane and Peter stared at each other. What were they going to do now?

Finally Peter said, "I guess we'll have to go in and get him."

Jane didn't like the idea. Neither did Peter. He couldn't help remembering what Mr. Krautkopf had said. But there was nothing else to do. They walked to the gate and pushed it. It was locked.

They walked on, peering in to see if they could get a glimpse of the Lieutenant. At last they got around to the back of the house. There the fence stopped, and there was a path leading to a porch.

Peter hesitated. He couldn't see anybody. There

was a vine hanging over the porch and covering it like a curtain. The vine was covered with little yellow-and-white flowers, and some bees were buzzing among them, but otherwise it was very quiet. He looked at Jane.

She was looking at him to see what he was going to do. It was up to him to do *something*. Even if the old lady came and chased them, they had to get their dog.

"Come on," said Peter. He walked up the path. Jane followed. The gravel crunched under their feet. They walked to the foot of the porch steps, and there at the top stood the Lieutenant! He looked down at them and wagged his little tail and barked his baby bark. "Yap! Yap!"

From a corner of the porch they could hear a dog growling. But it sounded like an old dog, not a pup.

"Here, Lieutenant," said Peter. "Come here!" But the puppy wouldn't come. He barked some more, and the other dog growled.

Then a lady appeared at the door. She was tall and thin and wore a blue cotton dress and a big apron, and her hair was pulled up in a bun on top of her head.

She looked surprised to see the children, and then

she looked at the Lieutenant and seemed even more surprised.

"Yes?" she said. "What did you want, children?"

Her voice was sweet, and not a bit cross.

"We—we came for our dog," Peter said. "He ran away from us and he's right there on the porch. Do you mind if we take him?"

"Oh!" she said. "Is the puppy yours? Wait a minute. If you come up here my dog may not like it." And she came out on the porch and picked up the Lieutenant and handed him down to Peter.

"Thank you," said Peter. He waited for a moment, hoping she would say something about coming in, or at least ask them what their names were, but she didn't.

"Well, good-by," said Peter, and he and Jane turned and started back to the street.

The Lieutenant turned his head and whined once or twice and wriggled, but Peter told him he had jumped ship and would be court-martialed if it happened again. The puppy licked his hand and went to sleep.

The children hurried home.

"I guess that was the lady Mr. Krautkopf was telling us about," said Peter. "But she wasn't cross, the way he said."

"I wish she had asked us to come in," said Jane. "Why didn't you talk to her more?"

"I couldn't think of anything to say," said Peter.

"Neither could I," said Jane, hurrying to keep up with him.

Suddenly she stopped. "You know what?" she

exclaimed. "I just thought of something! I didn't pay any attention at the time, but as we were going away—I saw the clothesline!"

Peter looked at her as though she had suddenly turned silly.

"The clothesline! Well, what about it?"

"Didn't you see what was on it?" asked Jane. "It's a clue!"

"No, I didn't," said Peter. "Clothes, I suppose. That's what you generally find on a clothesline."

"Of course," said Jane, "but there were two pairs of dungarees and some polo shirts."

"Well, what of it?" Peter asked impatiently.

"Well, don't you see," insisted Jane, "they were about the size we would wear."

Peter nodded. "By gum!" he said. "There must be some kids in that house!"

But how could they find out?

CHAPTER 4

The Jessups

All during lunch Peter and Jane kept discussing the matter of the clothesline and wondering how they could find out who else lived in the big house besides the lady in the blue dress. Peter thought they ought to stand around outside the fence and watch to see who came out. Jane didn't think that would be nice. Finally Mother heard them talking and asked what it was all about. When they told her, she said to stay away from there because the lady wouldn't want to be bothered. She said she would try to find out from the neighbors whether there were any children there or not.

After lunch Mother had to go marketing, and Peter and Jane went along to get a collar and leash for the Lieutenant so that he wouldn't run away again before he could be trained to obey.

They left the twins next door with Mrs. Mac-Dermott. She was a very nice person, and didn't seem to mind having a couple of extra babies left in her yard. Of course Mother was going to mind Teddy and Joany MacDermott when their mother went to market.

When the children got to the hardware store, the first thing they did was to look in the window for the other puppies. They were gone. Peter and Jane went inside, and the hardware-store man, whose name was Mr. Bunch, recognized them and asked how they were getting along with the Lieutenant. He patted the puppy and helped find a collar for him, though most of the collars were too big. Even the smallest one was rather loose on his neck, but Mr. Bunch said he would grow up to it. Then they got a bright-red leash, and Mr. Bunch gave them a little booklet all about how to take care of dogs. He told them to be sure to give the puppy enough water to drink, and not to take him out in the heat of the day because he was only a baby. Peter and Jane would have been glad to stand there all afternoon talking to Mr. Bunch if he had not had some other customers.

At last they tore themselves away. Mother was

waiting for them outside, and Peter put the Lieutenant down and tried to get him to walk along on his new red leash. But he sat down on the sidewalk and tried to bite it off. He didn't like it.

Peter was just about to pick him up when along came two children, a boy of about eleven and a girl somewhat younger. They were barefoot, and both had very light hair, almost white. And they were both wearing dungarees.

Jane and Peter gave them a friendly smile, but they didn't smile back. They both looked as mad as

if they had been fighting and they glared at Jane and Peter and walked past them into the store. Just as they were going up the steps, the Lieutenant made a leap at the boy, and let out a loud yap. But the boy just looked at him and pressed his lips together as if it made him madder than ever.

That made Peter pretty mad, too, but apparently Mother didn't notice it.

"Why, look," she said, "there are a couple of children your age! Why don't you see if you can get acquainted with them?"

"But Mother!" Peter protested. "How can we? We don't know where they live or anything."

"Oh, that's nothing," said Mother. "We can wait till they come out. I'll speak to them if you like."

"No, thanks, Mother," said Peter.

And Jane said, "Let's go home. The Lieutenant wants a drink." So they got away, but Mother looked rather disappointed.

Peter couldn't help thinking that it was funny that even Mother, who was the most understanding of parents, thought that simply because a child was your own age, you could just walk over to him and say, "Hey, let's get acquainted."

Why, after the way those kids had behaved, he didn't care if he never saw them again. When he talked to Jane about it, she felt the same way.

They went home and Jane read the little book about dogs, and spent an hour or two with Peter teaching the Lieutenant to heel, but the puppy had as much idea of discipline as a June bug. He just wore himself out pulling on the leash. He'd forget he had it on, and make a dash at some blade of grass, and then the collar would pull him up short and he'd sit down looking surprised.

At last evening came, and they got out the hose and sprinkled the lawn and helped Mother put the twins to bed, and finally went to bed themselves.

Just before taps, Jane said, "Well, tomorrow I'll see if I can find out where the library is around here."

And Peter said, "I guess I'll work on my ship model." But he was really wondering whether the whole summer was going to be like this—just minding babies and watering the lawn and working on a ship model.

The next day was hotter even than before. Mother put a big pan of water in the back yard and put the twins out in it with just their pants on, and let them splash. Peter and Jane had to be careful

not to let the babies drink any of the water. It kept them so busy that they didn't pay much attention to the Lieutenant, and suddenly Jane looked around and shouted, "Where is he?"

Peter jumped up and looked for him, but he was gone.

He ran to the front yard and looked up and down the street. Far away he could see a small black spot bounding along the pavement in the direction of the big house with the green trees.

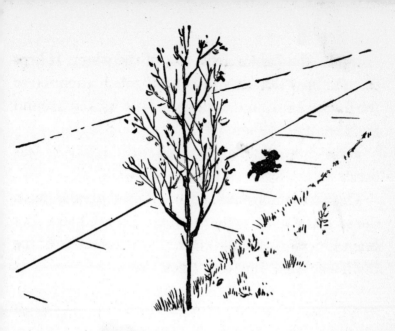

"He's running away!" Peter shouted. "Jane! Mind the twins! I've got to go after him!"

He ran as fast as he could, but the pup had a head start. By the time Peter reached the iron fence, the Lieutenant was gone. There was nothing to do but go around to the back and ask the lady again if he could have him.

He followed the fence to its end and then, instead of walking on the gravel, he stepped on the grass, because it was cooler. He was hot and sweaty from running and it was a relief to be in the shade.

51

His feet made no sound on the soft grass, and he could hear voices. One of them was the lady's.

"Now, Stephen," she was saying, "you know that isn't fair."

Then a boy's voice said angrily, "Well, if they can't take care of him they don't deserve him!"

And then another angry voice, which sounded like a girl's, said, "That's right! Taking him out in such heat and pulling him along the sidewalk!"

Peter's face got red. They were talking about him! He marched to the foot of the steps, making as much noise as he could. The voices stopped.

The lady in the blue dress was sitting in a chair with a low stool in front of her, on which was a wooden bucket. Beside her were the two children Peter and Jane had seen in front of the hardware store. The boy had the Lieutenant in his arms and was patting him.

For a moment nobody said a word. They all just stared at each other, and Peter was getting madder and madder.

Finally he said, "Excuse me, but my dog ran away again. Could I have him, if you don't mind?"

The two children didn't answer. They just looked angrily at Peter and then at the lady.

52

Then the lady said, very politely, "Oh, yes! You're the boy who was here yesterday. Won't you come up and sit down?"

Peter didn't want to do that. But he went up anyhow and said, "I'll just take the pup and not bother you any more."

"I'm Miss Jessup," said the lady, "and these children are my niece and nephew, Stephen and Katherine. We call her Kate."

"My name's Peter Bowman," said Peter. "And now could I just have my——"

"Well, we just wanted to speak to you a minute about the dog," said Miss Jessup.

"About the dog!" said Peter, wondering what this was all about. "Why, he's my dog."

"Well, you see," the lady explained, "he used to be ours."

Peter was flabbergasted. "Yours!" he said. "But Dad got him from Mr. Bunch, the hardware man."

"Yes," said Miss Jessup, "Mr. Bunch is an old friend of ours. We asked him to sell Bessie's puppies for us."

At that an old black dog got up from the corner and came toward Peter and sniffed him.

'This is Bessie," said Miss Jessup.

Peter patted her and Bessie wagged her tail.

"And we'd like to be sure that the puppies are treated kindly," said Miss Jessup. "Kate and Stephen seemed to think that since this one ran away, perhaps he isn't happy."

"But of course we treat him kindly," Peter said. "We wanted a puppy. We're crazy about him."

"They were dragging him!" Kate said, looking as if she might cry. "On the hot sidewalk!"

"We were not!" Peter exclaimed. "We carried him all the way. I just put him down to try the leash and he jumped at you. And I can't help it if it's hot. We haven't got a lot of nice trees like yours."

Then the boy got mad. "Well, you would have if they hadn't all been cut down," he shouted.

"Cut what down?" Peter shouted back. This was the silliest argument he had ever got into.

"The trees!" the boy yelled at him. "Aunt Matilda's the only one who had the sense not to——"

They were all ready to get into a fight when Miss Jessup interrupted. "Stephen! I'm ashamed of you!" she said.

Stephen stopped talking and got very red. He held out the Lieutenant and said, "Here, he's yours, you might as well take him."

Peter took the Lieutenant. The puppy stuck his face up and licked Peter's nose and thumped his little tail against Peter's stomach.

"Well, he seems to like you," said Miss Jessup. "Now suppose you all sit down and take turns helping me turn this freezer."

Stephen sat on the floor and took hold of the handle that stuck up out of the wooden bucket and started to turn it.

None of the three children looked at each other. Peter wanted to go home, but he was curious about the wooden bucket.

"What is that?" he asked at last.

"An ice-cream freezer," said Miss Jessup.

"An ice-cream freezer!" Peter said. "My mother makes ice cream in the refrigerator."

"Well, we have none," said Miss Jessup.

"You haven't!" exclaimed Peter. He had never heard of anybody who had no refrigerator, especially people who lived in such a grand house as this seemed to be. Why, even in their little bungalow, the Bowmans had a big new refrigerator!

"No, we haven't!" Stephen snapped. "We haven't got such fancy new things!"

"Stephen!" said Miss Jessup. And Stephen

pressed his lips together and turned the handle faster and faster.

"Now it's Peter's turn," said Miss Jessup, and Peter sat down and began to crank the handle.

And as he cranked, Miss Jessup gently asked him questions about himself, and pretty soon he was telling all about how the Bowmans had happened to move to Sea View Gardens, and how they might have liked a bigger house, but the bungalow was the best they could afford. Then he told how Father had left them the Lieutenant as their sailing orders, and how he and Jane were earning their bicycles by baby-sitting every morning with the twins.

When he mentioned the twins, Kate said "Oh!" and her eyes got big and round.

"Kate likes babies," Miss Jessup explained.

Then Peter found out that Stephen and Kate had no father or mother, but were living with Miss Jessup, who was their great-aunt. They hadn't wanted to sell all the puppies, but their aunt said one dog was all they could keep, and that was why they had felt so badly about seeing the Lieutenant mistreated (as they thought).

And before Peter knew it, they were all talking as though they had been friends for a long time.

56

They took turns cranking the ice-cream freezer

Pretty soon the handle became so hard to turn that Peter thought his arm would break off and just then Miss Jessup said, "It's done."

Kate went for some dishes, and Miss Jessup took the lid off the bucket and inside was some of the most wonderful-looking pink ice cream Peter had ever seen. Miss Jessup filled the dishes and Kate passed them around.

Peter took a spoonful. Was it good!

"Boy!" he said. "This is the best ice cream I ever ate. It's got real strawberries in it!"

"Stephen raised the berries in his garden," said Miss Jessup.

"He did!" said Peter. "Boy, you must be some gardener!"

"Oh, nothing much," said Stephen modestly. "Want to see the garden?"

Peter could see that the garden was what Stephen was interested in, just as he liked ship models.

"You bet!" he said. But suddenly he remembered that he had left Jane with the twins. "Look," he said, "can I come back this afternoon and bring my sister? I left her at home and she'll be mad."

"Sure," said Stephen.

"Oh, yes," said Kate.

"Okay. I have to go now, but I'll be back." And he jumped up and picked up the Lieutenant.

"Thanks for the ice cream," he called over his shoulder as he ran down the walk.

"Don't forget to come back!" Stephen and Kate called after him.

CHAPTER 5

Inside Sea View

Peter ran home as fast as he could. He couldn't wait to tell Jane.

Jane was quite annoyed at being left alone with the twins for so long, so Peter explained that he couldn't help it, he had been eating ice cream.

Of course that made her madder than ever, so to calm her down Peter told all that had happened.

"And now we're acquainted with the Jessups," he finished, "and we're invited to come back today."

That made it all right with Jane. "Goody!" she gurgled. "Now maybe we'll get to see the secret staircase."

"Don't be silly," said Peter. "You and your secret staircases." But secretly he was hoping they *would* see what the house was like inside.

They put the Lieutenant in Peter's room and shut the door so that he couldn't get out and run away again. He howled a bit, but after Jane went in and gave him a biscuit and a drink of water he curled up and went to sleep. He was tired.

As soon as the lunch dishes were put away, Peter and Jane set out, taking the Lieutenant with them. Stephen and Kate were waiting for them on the back porch.

"This is my sister Jane," said Peter.

"Hi," said Stephen.

Kate stood behind her brother and smiled. She seemed bashful. She didn't look a bit like the angry girl Peter had seen that morning.

"What do you want to do?" Stephen asked.

"Oh!" said Jane. "Have you got a s——"

But Peter gave her a shove and she stopped in time. Peter was beginning to get tired of her secret staircases.

"Could we look at the garden?" he asked, knowing that that was what Stephen would like.

"Sure," said Stephen. "You can leave the pup on the porch with Bessie. He'll stay there."

Peter put the Lieutenant down and he waddled over and lay down beside his mother, who opened one eye and looked at him and then went back to sleep again.

Stephen led the way down a path toward the shed behind the house. Peter glanced at him now and then as they went. Stephen was taller than Peter, and thinner, and very serious looking. Once in a while he frowned as though he were worried about something, and an up-and-down wrinkle appeared in his forehead.

"Be careful," he said, as the path curved around a big flat stone. He stopped to see that nobody stumbled.

"What's that?" Jane asked.

"That's the well cover," he said.

"Have you got a well?" said Jane.

"Sure," said Stephen. "That's where we get our water."

Peter thought it was odd. He was quite sure the water in his house didn't come from a well, but from pipes in the ground. But he didn't say anything, for just then they heard a soft, clucking sound.

"Those are the chickens," said Kate.

"Chickens! Can we see them?" Jane asked.

"All right," said Stephen, "but you must be quiet and not frighten Abigail."

"Who's that?" Jane asked.

"That's our setting hen," said Stephen. "She's

sitting on ten eggs, and she might not like strangers coming in."

He opened the shed door gently and they stepped in. The sun streamed through the low windows in dusty streaks. Some black and brown hens lay snoozing in the sawdust on the floor. A few more were walking around remarking, "Cut-cut-cut," in sleepy voices.

"There's Abigail," Kate whispered, pointing to a black hen sitting in a box fastened to the wall. Abigail stuck her head out and looked at the visitors.

Suddenly there was a terrific noise. A hen jumped down out of a box, yelling, "Cut-cut-cut-cudaaaaaakut!" She ran around the floor as if a fire engine were after her.

"What's wrong with her?" Peter asked.

"Oh, she just laid an egg," said Stephen. He walked over to the box and came back with the egg in his hand.

"Here, you can have it," he said to Peter.

The egg was brown and smooth, and still warm. Peter turned it over in his hand. He looked up at Stephen and Stephen looked back at him. Peter understood that Stephen was sorry he had been angry and wanted to be friends.

Peter grinned. Then he pointed to the noisy hen and said, "I thought we were supposed to be quiet in here."

"Oh, Abigail doesn't mind that," said Stephen. And sure enough, the setting hen didn't pay the least attention to the racket.

They went out again and Stephen shut the door carefully. He led them along the path to the vegetable garden. Here plants were growing in neat rows. There was a patch of corn, about knee-high, and some beans growing on poles, and some tomato plants with little green tomatoes on them.

"Is that your garden? It's keen!" said Peter.

Stephen said, "Well, of course Aunt Matilda helped with the planting, but I take care of it." It was easy to see he was proud of the garden. "Here's the strawberry bed," he said.

He held out some red berries in the palm of his hand to Peter and Jane. Peter took two and ate them. They were delicious.

Suddenly Jane called, "Oh! Look at that!"

She was pointing at a small brown goat that was looking at them over a fence. "A goat!" Jane exclaimed. "Isn't it sweet!"

"All right, don't make so much noise," said Peter, wishing his sister were not quite so excitable.

"Ma-a-a!" said the goat.

"That's Taffy," said Kate. She plucked a spray of ivy from the wall of the shed and brought it to the goat, who began to nibble it. Kate scratched the goat's head gently.

"She doesn't like to be here all alone," she said. "She wants to have company. Don't you, Taffy?"

"Well, why don't you tie her near the house, then?" Peter asked. "I should think a pet would like to be where people are."

"Well, she isn't just a pet," said Stephen. "She has to stay in her pasture and eat grass."

"What do you mean, she isn't a pet?" Peter asked. "What do you keep her for?"

"For milk," said Stephen. "Let's go back."

They started back toward the house. "Ma-a-a!" the goat called after them.

"Cut-cut-cut!" the hens cackled from their house.

And the tomato plants sent up a tempting odor as the sun blazed down on them.

"Could we have a drink?" Jane asked when they got back to the porch.

"Sure," said Steve. (Peter had begun to call him Steve by this time.) "Come into the kitchen."

They followed him in. Peter stared about him. It was the strangest kitchen he had ever been in.

First of all, there was a huge black stove with a kind of hood over the top. There was a fire in it, and the kitchen was as hot as a furnace. Something smelled awfully good. Peter sniffed and looked around. There were four loaves of freshly baked bread on the table.

Steve gave each of them a glass of water from the pump

"Oh!" said Kate. "Aunt Matilda made the bread. I told her I'd help her but she did it while we were out."

"She says it's too hot for you in here," Steve said. "You know that. Now come on and get the glasses."

Kate got some glasses out of the cupboard and Peter looked around for the refrigerator. His mother always kept some water in there when it was hot. But there was no refrigerator. He remembered now that Miss Jessup had said they had none. Then he looked for the sink. It was opposite the stove, and it was made of black iron, and instead of faucets it had a pump! Steve seized the handle and pumped it up and down and a stream of water ran out. Each of them filled a glass. The water was ice-cold and tasted wonderful.

"Where does the water come from?" Peter asked.

"From the well," said Steve.

"But where do you keep the milk and butter?" said Peter.

"Down cellar," said Steve. "Want to see it?"

And he opened a door that led to a flight of steps. The children went down. It was cool and dim down there, and smelled damp but nice. On a long table against one wall was a stone tub with a lid, several

68

pitchers covered with napkins, and a bowl of eggs. Peter walked over and put his egg on the table.

"I'll leave it here till we go," he said.

A blast of heat came at them as they climbed the stairs back to the kitchen.

"Come on out," said Steve, starting outdoors.

But Jane had caught a glimpse of something through another door. "Oh, Stephen," she said, "what's that wonderful thing hanging on the wall in there? Could we see it?" Jane was always seeing something wonderful.

"Yes, I guess so," said Steve. And he led them through the door into a dining room. It was a beautiful room with white paneled walls. There was a polished table in the middle, and a sideboard with silver teapots at one side, and a china closet full of blue-and-gold dishes. In the middle of the ceiling was a crystal chandelier, and on one of the walls was the thing that Jane had seen—a huge red silk dragon.

"Our great-grandfather brought it from China," said Steve.

"Oh, really? When?" Jane asked.

"Oh, when Aunt Matilda was little, I guess," said Steve.

"What did he go to China for?"

"He was a ship captain," said Steve. "He had his own ship."

"He did!" Peter burst out. "Wow! That's keen! I never thought I'd know anybody that had their own ship, I mean his great-grandfather had his own ship, I mean———"

He was getting mixed up in his excitement.

"You want to see what the ship looked like?" Steve asked.

"*Do* I!" exclaimed Peter. "You have a picture of it, or something?"

"Come on, I'll show you," said Steve, smiling with pleasure, and he took them through a doorway into a wide hall. On the walls were spears and shields and strange embroidered tapestries, a lace fan, and a ship's clock. A wide, curving staircase with shiny bannisters led to the second floor. Peter wondered what was up there, but Steve didn't go up. He led them past all these things into a room that was even larger than the dining room. Their sneakers sank into a soft rug.

The shutters were closed, and only narrow streaks of sunlight filtered through. The furniture was cov-

ered with muslin slip covers. On a marble-topped table was a shiny pink shell. In a corner stood a glass cabinet filled with little carved animals of ivory and wood.

Over the fireplace hung a red velvet curtain, and in front of this, on the mantel, stood a little ship.

Peter walked across the room and stood in front of it without saying anything. It was beautiful. It stood on a polished black base on which were carved the words *Flying Swallow*. Its hull was of brown wood, smoothly polished. It had three masts, and it stood with all its little sails set as if it were all ready to catch the first breeze. Every rope and shroud was in place, every lifeboat and hatch cover.

"Golly!" Peter said at last. "She's swell!"

"That's a model of my great-grandfather's ship," said Steve. "He made her."

"You mean the ship or the model?" Peter asked.

"Well, the model," said Steve. "He couldn't make the ship. But he designed her. Same as he designed Sea View."

"Designed what?" Peter asked.

"Sea View," said Steve. "This house."

"Oh!" said Peter and Jane, both together. "You mean your house is called Sea View?"

"Sure," said Steve. Kate nodded her head.

"But then is that why this place is called Sea View Gardens?" Jane asked.

"I guess so," said Steve, scowling angrily.

"You mean your aunt let that real-estate man use the name of your house?" said Peter.

"No, she didn't," said Steve. "He just took it."

Peter could see why Steve was angry. "Why, that's not right!" he exclaimed indignantly. "That's just like stealing!"

"That's what *I* think," said Steve.

"It's a gyp to call it Sea View Gardens anyhow," said Peter. "You can't see the sea from any of it."

"Well, you can see it from our house," said Steve. "That's why it's called Sea View."

Peter and Jane were enchanted. This place was getting more wonderful every minute.

"You mean," said Peter, "from that little square box on the top of the house?"

"That's the cupola," said Steve. "Sure. That's why my great-grandfather built it—so he could see his ship at anchor. See, here's his telescope. He used to keep it up there." And he lifted a long black tube from a stand by the window.

Peter ran his fingers gently along its smooth,

worn leather. "Could—could we go up there?" he stammered. "I mean, if your aunt doesn't mind? Could you really see ships out there on the sea?"

"Of course," said Steve. "Come on, we'll go up." He started toward the hall, carrying the telescope.

They followed him up the stairs. There was a wide hall on the second floor off which bedroom doors opened.

They went up to a third floor where the doors were all shut. It was very hot and close up here.

"These are the attics," said Steve.

He led them up a third flight of stairs, a narrow winding flight that didn't go to a landing at all but opened straight into the floor of a room.

Peter gasped. The view was like nothing he had ever seen before. There were windows on all four sides. They looked down on the tops of the trees and on the roofs of little houses, red and blue and green. And far off was the ocean. It sparkled in the sunlight and boats floated on its blue surface, within the shelter of a curved bay.

"That's Sea Harbor down there," said Steve.

A steamer crawled slowly across the horizon, leaving a thin trail of smoke behind it in the air. Steve raised the telescope to his eye and adjusted it.

"Here, take a look," he said to Peter.

Peter held it to his right eye. The steamer, which had looked so tiny, became a real ship now. He could see men moving on her deck. He could even see the name, *City of Savannah,* on her bows.

"Let me see too!" Jane demanded, jumping impatiently up and down.

Steve had opened a couple of windows, and the wind blew in. It smelled of the sea, fresh and salty. Peter drew a deep breath. Long ago, he thought, there would have been sailing ships out there.

Suddenly, far below, a ship's clock chimed. Ding! Ding!

"Oh, what time is that?" Jane asked.

"Two bells, five o'clock," said Steve.

"We have to go," said Peter. "We've got to help Mother with the twins while she gets supper."

They ran down the stairs. "Come again tomorrow," Kate said, as they went. "Come early."

"We can't. We have to mind the twins in the morning. We'll come after lunch," said Jane.

They went through the dining room and out the kitchen door. Miss Jessup was sitting in her rocking chair on the back porch shelling peas for supper.

"Have you had a pleasant afternoon?" she asked.

"Oh, wonderful!" said Jane enthusiastically. "This is the most wonderful house I ever saw! Stephen and Kate said we could come again to-morrow."

"Please do," said Miss Jessup.

Peter picked up the Lieutenant and they started for home. As they reached the sidewalk they turned to wave good-by. Suddenly they almost bumped into a short, stout man who was getting out of a small green car.

"Please look where you are going," he said crossly, and walked past them up the gravel path.

"Why, that was Mr. Krautkopf," said Jane.

"It's funny he didn't recognize us," said Peter. "But what's he doing at Sea View?"

"I don't know," said Jane.

CHAPTER 6

Beans, Marbles and a Yellow Satin Ribbon

Of course Peter and Jane could hardly talk about anything but Sea View, and they didn't see how they would live until the next afternoon, when they could go back there. But the evening and the next morning and lunch time passed somehow, and at last it was time to start.

"Remember," Mother said, as they were starting out, "don't bother Miss Jessup. And be sure to invite the Jessup children to come to visit us."

"I don't see why they should want to," said Peter. "It's much nicer there."

"Just the same," said Mother, "invite them to lunch tomorrow."

"Okay," said Peter, picking up the Lieutenant. He and Jane hurried down the street.

"What do you suppose we will do today?" Jane asked, skipping beside him.

77

"We could play tag in the garden," said Peter.

"We could look at the things in the parlor," said Jane, "if they would let us."

But when they arrived, the Jessup family was busy on the back porch, cutting up beans. There was a bushel basket of them.

"Hello," Steve said. "We can't play yet, we have to cut beans."

"What are all those for?" Peter asked. "Are you having company?"

"Of course not," said Kate. "They're from the garden. We're going to can them for winter."

Peter thought it would take forever to cut up all those beans, but Jane was not discouraged.

"We'll help too," she said. "That will make it quicker."

Kate got two extra knives and they all went to work, cutting off the tops and tails and chopping the beans, while Miss Jessup went into the kitchen and began cooking the ones that were ready.

"It's a hot day for cooking," said Peter.

"Yes," said Steve, "but the beans won't wait. They're ripe now and if we wait they'll spoil, and what will we eat next winter?"

And he chopped harder than ever.

The beans took a long time, and when at last they were finished, the four of them were so tired that they just went into the front yard and sat down on the grass.

It was nice and cool there. The breeze swayed the tall grass. It swung the purple flowers of the vine that hung over the front porch, and Peter noticed that a corner of the porch roof was broken. He wondered why Miss Jessup or Steve didn't do something about it. He thought he could fix it if he could only get up there. Once he had helped Dad fix a roof. But he didn't like to say anything about it.

Peter looked up at the trees. Several of them were very tall and straight, with just a few branches at the top.

"Those look like ship masts," he said to Steve.

"That's what they used to use them for," said Steve. "They're Norway poplars. My great-grandfather planted them."

"And what kind of tree is that over there?" Peter asked. He pointed to a very thick tree with flaky yellowish bark quite close to the side of the house.

"It's a sycamore," said Steve. "Before they cut down all the other trees around here, it used to be the fattest tree in the neighborhood."

"Then it's still the fattest, I guess," said Peter, and he took out a ball and threw it against the side of the tree. It bounced back, and the Lieutenant, who had been playing with the girls, ran after it and brought it back to him. He threw it again and the puppy ran after it and brought it back.

Then he tossed it high into the tree. He expected it to come down on the other side, but it didn't. The little dog ran all around looking for it. But the ball had disappeared.

"What happened to it?" he demanded.

Steve laughed.

"I guess it's stuck in the tree," he said.

"How could it be?" Peter asked. He got up and went to look at the tree.

There was a ladder made of thin strips of wood nailed to the trunk.

"It's got steps!" he said. "Can we go up?"

"Well, I don't know," said Steve, wiggling one of the steps. "I'm not sure they're all strong enough to climb on. It's a long time since I've been up there."

"I can fix them. Just get a hammer," said Peter.

Steve went to the house and soon came back with a hammer and nails. Peter climbed up, knocking in extra nails where they were needed. Steve followed him up.

There was a fine flat place in the crotch of the tree, big enough for three people to sit in. A couple of boards had been laid across to make a floor.

"This is good," said Peter. "It's a crow's nest. I'm the lookout." And he shaded his eyes with his hand and pretended to peer out across the ocean.

"Whale off the starboard bow!" he shouted. "Thar she blows!"

"Yap! Yap!" barked the whale, running around down on the ground.

"Heave hard on the topgallant mizzenmast!" Peter yelled. "Belay there!"

"Stop that!" Jane called. "You're getting the Lieutenant all excited."

Peter sat down and looked for his ball.

"Where did it go?" he asked.

"I guess it fell in between these planks," said Steve. He put his hand down.

"I can't reach it," he said. "There's a deep hole in there."

Peter put his hand in. "We'd better pry up one of these boards," he said.

He stuck the prong of his hammer under the edge

Peter picked up a handful of the stuff and sifted it

of a board and pulled. With a great creak of rusty nails the board gave way and both boys looked in.

In the crotch of the tree was a heap of broken nut shells, dead leaves, chewed up acorns and sawdust. On top of this heap was the ball. Peter put it in his pocket.

"What's all this stuff?" he asked.

"Looks like a squirrel's nest," said Steve.

"But such a lot!" said Peter. "Let's clean it out."

He picked up a handful of the stuff and sifted it between his fingers. Steve took some too. It floated out into the air like a cloud.

"Stop that!" Kate called. "You're getting it all over us!"

"Get out of the way then," said Peter. "We're swabbing down the deck!"

They worked harder and faster, scooping out sawdust and throwing it down.

Suddenly Peter stopped. "Avast there!" he said. "I found something."

"What is it?" Steve asked.

Peter held out his hand. In it was a round ball, about an inch in diameter, black with dirt.

"That's a funny kind of nut," he said.

Steve scraped it with his nail. Under the dirt it

83

was white. It looked like china.

"It's a marble," he said.

"That's a funny marble," said Peter. "I never saw one as big as that. What makes you think it's a marble?"

"It looks like some marbles my grandfather had," said Steve. "I've got a few in the house. Only this is bigger than the others."

"But what's it doing in the tree?" Peter asked.

"That's what I'd like to know," said Steve.

"Maybe a squirrel thought it was a nut," said Peter. "Then when he found he couldn't eat it, he left it here."

"Let's see if there's anything else here," said Steve, beginning to dig again. "Wait, maybe we threw something down." And he shouted over the side to the girls to look around on the ground. They began crawling around on their knees, searching in the grass, while the boys in the tree picked up handfuls of sawdust and sifted it carefully.

"What are you looking for?" Peter asked.

"Well, I—I don't know exactly," said Steve. Then he picked up something with his thumb and forefinger. "What do you think this is?" he asked.

At first Peter thought it was a dead leaf. It was so

dry and brown and brittle that it seemed about to crumble into dust. But when he looked more closely he saw that it wasn't a leaf.

"It looks like one of those bows that girls wear on their braids," he said.

"That's what I thought," said Steve, "but what would *that* be doing in a squirrel's nest?"

"Maybe a lady squirrel wore it on her tail," suggested Peter.

Steve smiled. Then he put the board back.

"Come on," he said. "We'd better show this to Aunt Matilda." He started down the ladder, and ran for the kitchen, with Peter and the girls after him.

Aunt Matilda was just taking the last of the jars out of the preserving kettle. Her face was red with the heat and her white hair hung down in wisps. She wiped her forehead with a handkerchief.

"Now, children, this is no place for you," she said.

"Look what we found," said Steve, holding out the marble but keeping the bow behind him.

Aunt Matilda took the little ball. "Where did you get that?" she asked.

"In the sycamore," said Steve.

Aunt Matilda rubbed it with a wet cloth. The dirt came off and showed a white china ball.

85

"It's one of Thomas's marbles," she said, turning it over in her hand.

"I never saw such a big marble," said Peter.

"It's a shooter," she said. "You children don't use big shooters any more, do you?"

"No," said Peter.

Steve was rummaging in a little drawer in the kitchen cabinet. He took something out and showed it to Peter. It was a white china marble, just like the big one but much smaller.

"See," he said, "here's one I found once in the parlor sofa. And I've got a couple more up in my room."

"But how did the shooter get up in the sycamore?" Peter wondered.

Aunt Matilda smiled. "Thomas was always losing his marbles," she said. "We used to find them all over the house. He liked to climb up in that sycamore, too. So it's not surprising he lost some there."

"Did you climb up in the tree too, Aunt Matilda?" Steve asked.

"Oh, no," said Aunt Matilda. "I wasn't allowed to climb trees when I was a little girl."

"Then wasn't this yours?" Steve asked, bringing out the bow.

Aunt Matilda had not been much surprised about the shooter, but when she saw the bow she was really astonished. She sat down in a chair and turned a little pale.

"Where did you get that?" she demanded.

"In the sycamore," said Steve.

Kate and Jane leaned closer to get a look at it.

"It looks like a hair bow," said Jane.

"But it's awful old and dirty," said Kate.

"It looks to me," said Aunt Matilda, "like the bow that went with my yellow satin dress."

At this Kate's eyes opened wide. "You mean the satin dress in the picture?" she asked.

"Yes," said Aunt Matilda, thinking back. "Mother scolded me for losing the bow. She had such a time matching the ribbon. And I was sure Thomas hid it to tease me. He was a dreadful tease, that boy."

"But that isn't yellow," said Kate.

Aunt Matilda peered at the thing in the palm of her hand.

"No, it isn't," she said. "It wouldn't be, after all these years in a tree. It's amazing that it's held together this long. Look, you can still see the little flowers woven into the silk."

The children bent their heads and squinted at the little brown ribbon. Sure enough, there did seem to be a pattern in it.

"May we go and look at the picture, Aunt Matilda?" Kate asked. "May we see if it really is the yellow bow?"

Aunt Matilda nodded. She got up and pushed the preserving kettle to the back of the stove. Then she went through the dining room, through the hall and into the darkened parlor. The children followed her. She went to the window and unfastened a shutter.

Then she walked to the mantel where the red velvet curtain hung, and pulled a cord which hung at the side of the curtain. The curtain parted, and there was a large painting.

It was of a boy and a girl. Their hair was light and their eyes were blue. They looked surprisingly like Steve and Kate.

"That's Aunt Matilda," said Kate. "And the boy is grandfather."

Nobody else spoke. They just stood and looked at the picture. The boy was dressed in velvet, and he held a small ship model in his hands. On his shoulder a monkey was perched.

The girl wore a yellow satin dress. In her hands

was a small black lacquer box. Her hair was braided and on each braid was a yellow satin bow.

Aunt Matilda held up the dusty brown bow.

"I was right," she said. "It *is* my bow."

It was hard to believe that the crumbling brown thing was the same as the fresh bright ribbon on the little girl's hair, or that the old lady had been that little girl. Peter didn't like to think about it.

He went up close to the picture. "Is that the *Flying Swallow?*" he asked.

"It is," said Aunt Matilda. "The picture was a surprise for my father. So Thomas was to hold the ship model."

"And was that a real monkey?" Peter asked.

"Yes, indeed," said Aunt Matilda. "Father brought him home from India. He was Thomas' monkey, but he liked my mother best. He followed her everywhere."

She sat down on the sheet-covered sofa and looked down at the bow in her hands. "It seems a very long time ago," she murmured. Then she sighed. The four children stood and waited.

"Tell about how the picture was painted," said Kate at last.

"You know perfectly well, Kate," said Aunt Matilda. "But of course Peter and Jane don't. Well, I'll tell them. . . . Father was away on a voyage," she went on, "and suddenly Mother had the idea of having our picture painted. So she got the painter in. He was a famous painter. And every afternoon we had to stand still for an hour or two while he painted. It was very tiresome. Thomas wouldn't stand still unless he could have the monkey. And sometimes the monkey was hard to catch."

"He had a collar and chain," said Steve.

"Yes, but he was clever about getting loose," said Aunt Matilda. "And he'd climb all over the house. He led us a merry chase. There would be Mother and the maids, and Thomas and I, and the painter, all trying to get the monkey down from the chandelier or the porch roof, or wherever he was perched."

"The painter too?" Peter asked.

"Well, he couldn't paint while his subjects were chasing a monkey. Mother could usually catch him at last. He would come down for her, and she would snap the chain on his collar and give him to Thomas. And then of course I had to have the box."

"Tell about the box," Kate begged.

"You've heard the story many times, child," said Aunt Matilda. "It was Mother's jewel box. Father

91

brought it from China the time he brought the red dragon. Mother kept her rings in it. And I wanted to hold it. I liked the feel of it. It was so smooth."

"You mean you held the box with the rings in it?" Jane asked. Her black eyes shone. This was the kind of story she liked.

"Oh, no," said Aunt Matilda. "She kept the box in a special drawer in her bedroom. And she would go up and take the rings out and bring the box down for me to hold. And when we were through posing for that afternoon she would take the box back upstairs and put the rings back in it and put it away."

"Why didn't she wear the rings?" Jane asked.

"They were very beautiful and valuable," said Aunt Matilda. "One was a ruby and the other an emerald. She only wore them on special occasions."

"Like when great-grandfather came home?" Kate whispered.

"Yes. We had to hurry with the painting," said Aunt Matilda. "Father was expected home. Every day Mother would go up to the cupola and look for his ship. They anchored in the harbor, you know."

Peter said, "Yes. Steve told us. Did all the big ships come in there?"

"Yes, indeed," said Aunt Matilda. "Only fishing

boats come in there now, and the big boats steam right past. But in those days they anchored off the shore. And Mother knew, when she saw the *Flying Swallow* at anchor, that Father would be home before night."

"So what happened?" Peter exclaimed.

"The painter was painting, and Mother was up in the cupola, and suddenly she came running down and said, 'The ship is in! The ship is in! You must finish today!' And the painter hurried and painted some more, but we were so excited we couldn't sit still, so pretty soon he stopped and went home.

"And we had to keep our best clothes on because Father was coming, and Mother took the black lacquer box upstairs and then she came down crying, 'My rings are gone!' "

Steve and Kate had heard the story before, of course, so they weren't surprised, but Jane jumped.

Even Peter couldn't keep calm. "Her rings were gone!" he exclaimed. "What happened to them?"

Aunt Matilda shook her head. "We never found them," she said.

"But did you look everywhere?"

Aunt Matilda smiled. "Of course," she said. "We searched in every crack. We questioned everybody.

But they were gone."

"And what happened next?" Jane breathed.

"Well, then we heard horses' hoofs, and we knew Father was home. We ran out on the front porch, and there was his carriage coming up the drive, and Father got out and kissed us all. My, he did look handsome in his captain's uniform!"

"What did he say about the rings?" Peter asked.

"Well, he felt sorry. He helped look for them. But we never found them."

"And did he like the picture?" Kate asked.

"Yes, dear, he loved the picture," said Aunt Matilda. "He thought it was a wonderful surprise."

"But what about your bow?" said Jane. "When did you lose that?"

"Oh, I think that was the next day," said Aunt Matilda. "I was sure Thomas had taken it to tease me, and now you see I was right. He hid it in the sycamore, the naughty boy."

She sighed again, and stood up. She drew the curtain over the picture and closed the shutter.

"Well, it was a long time ago," she said, "and now it's time for chores." And she walked out into the hall. As the children followed her, the ship's clock struck four bells.

94

"Golly!" said Peter. "We have to run. We ought to be home now." Suddenly he remembered. "Could Steve and Kate come to lunch at our house tomorrow?" he asked.

"Why, of course," said Aunt Matilda. "That would be lovely."

But Steve shook his head. "We'll have more beans to do," he said. "There's another bushel that will be ready tomorrow."

Kate's face fell. "I was wishing we could see the twins," she whispered to Jane.

"I know what let's do," said Jane. "You come to lunch, and after lunch we'll all come back here and chop beans again."

"Why, that's very nice," said Aunt Matilda. "But I don't think you two should work so hard."

"Oh, we *love* it here," said Jane. "We don't mind working so long as we can be here."

CHAPTER 7

The Jessups Come to Visit

Stepping out into the afternoon sunlight, Peter felt as if he had been reading a story —a fascinating story about a world where there were no steamboats or water faucets or automobiles, where fathers went around the world in sailing ships and brought back Chinese dragons.

But if Jane had been excited about Sea View before, now she was twice as excited.

All the way home she kept saying, "I just *knew* there was a mystery about that place. Isn't it fun!"

All through supper she kept bursting out, "Oh, if only we can find the rings!"

"What makes you think we can find them?" Peter asked.

"Oh, they must be there somewhere," said Jane.

"I don't think so," said Peter. "Aunt Matilda said they looked everywhere."

"Well they must be some place where they didn't look, or they would have found them," said Jane.

"Mother, make her stop," said Peter. He wanted to think about the *Flying Swallow* lying at anchor out in the harbor, and Jane interfered.

His mother laughed. "Jane is going to be a writer," she said. "She just can't let go of a good story when she hears one, so we may as well let her talk. Anyway, I don't know how to stop her."

However, by the next morning Jane had run down somewhat, which was a good thing, as they had to get ready for the guests.

They rushed around tidying things up, putting away all the twins' stray rattles, blocks, balls, bibs and little shirts that were lying around. They washed the dishes. They put blue sunsuits on the twins, and brushed their hair, and Jane tied a little bow on Peggy so you could tell her apart from Johnny. Then they set the table, and soon it was time for the company to arrive. They went out and hung over the fence, and there were Steve and Kate coming down the street.

They were all slicked up too. Steve's hair was wet from brushing and Kate had on a dress instead of dungarees. It was a faded blue, and seemed rather

97

short for her. They were looking carefully at the house numbers as they went along, so as not to miss the Bowmans' house.

Peter and Jane ran out and waved to them, and the Lieutenant came out and jumped all over them.

Kate seemed very shy, and Steve was trying hard to be polite. Peter and Jane showed them around the garden first. There wasn't much to see, except one spindly little tree in the middle of the front lawn, and a few bushes stuck around, and the vine that Father had planted, and the seeds that Peter had put in, just starting to come up out of the bare earth. Steve was very polite and didn't say anything at all.

Then they went indoors. Mother had stopped typing and was getting lunch ready. She came to the door to greet them. She had on a new dress that Peter and Jane hadn't seen before. It was yellow, with no sleeves and a very wide skirt, and she looked very pretty.

She held out both hands and said, "My, I'm glad to see some young people around here. Peter and Jane have been having such fun at your house, and there are no other children around here except babies——"

98

"I like babies," Kate said, almost in a whisper.

"Well, you came to the right place," said Mother, for just then the twins came crawling across the floor like two puppies coming to greet the company.

Kate forgot all about her shyness. Her face lit up with a big smile, and she plopped down on her knees and tried to take them both in her arms at once. The twins climbed all over her and gurgled and laughed, and she talked baby talk to them. Then Jane sat down on the floor too, and there were girls and babies all over the place.

Peter saw that something had to be done. "Come on, Steve," he said, "I'll show you the rest of the place."

He took Steve to his room and showed him the models he had made, and his work bench, and the ship he was working on.

Then he showed him the rest of the house. It didn't take long. Peter felt that Steve couldn't be much interested in such a little house as this, after living at Sea View. But Steve was very much interested. He looked at the shiny faucets in the bathroom, and the automatic oil burner in the furnace room, and the smooth linoleum floors.

"Say," he said, "this house is pretty nice."

Then they went to the kitchen to see what Mother was doing about lunch, and when he saw the kitchen Steve behaved the way Kate had done when she saw the twins. Of course he didn't throw himself on the sink and kiss it, but he stood with his mouth open as if he thought it was perfectly wonderful. Peter had never before seen a boy act that way in a kitchen, and he couldn't understand what was wrong with him.

Steve walked around and looked at the electric stove and the refrigerator and the washing machine

Then he remembered his manners and said, "You have a very nice house, Mrs. Bowman."

"I'm glad you like it," said Mother. "I like it too, it's so convenient." And she opened the refrigerator and showed him the place where the frozen food was kept, and then she showed him the dish-washer, and how the washing machine worked, and the electric toaster and the ironer, and all he could say was "Gosh!"

Then lunch was ready and Mother called the girls. They came in, each carrying a twin. They put the twins in their high chairs. Kate fed Peggy and Jane fed Johnny, and the boys had no trouble feeding themselves.

Mother had really prepared a good lunch. There was chicken salad and corn muffins and malted milk.

Steve was especially impressed when Mother took the corn muffins out of the oven.

"Did you have the oven on all this time?" he asked.

"Yes," said Mother, "why?"

"Because we're having lunch right here in the kitchen and it isn't hot," said Steve.

Mother laughed and said, "That's the way these modern stoves are made. I waited a long time for mine, and I certainly appreciate it." And she gave the stove a pat.

"You certainly couldn't do that to our stove," said Kate, looking away from Peggy for a moment. "You'd burn yourself."

After lunch Mother and the girls put the twins to bed, and Peter and Steve stacked the dishes in the dish-washer. Steve had to stand there and watch through the little window while the dishes were being washed. Then the girls came in and of course Kate had to see too.

Now that she didn't have to keep her mind on the twins, she was able to pay some attention to the kitchen too, and she was just as impressed as Steve.

"This is wonderful!" Kate said, looking around. "If only Aunt Matilda could have one like this!"

"Yes, but you know what she'd say," said Steve. "She'd want to keep everything just the way it always was."

"I know, but think of a dish-washer!" said Kate.

The dish-washer had stopped now, after giving the dishes a final shower of hot water, but still they wanted to stand there and look at it.

"Come on," said Peter, "let's go out. I've been in the house all morning and I'm tired of it."

Kate and Steve had to watch the dish-washer

Steve was surprised. "You have?" he asked. "Why?"

"We were minding the twins," said Peter. "You know, I told you. To earn our bikes."

"Sure, but can't the twins go out?" Steve asked.

"Oh, no," said Jane. "Not on a day like this. It's a scorcher. It's too hot for them. We have to keep them in."

"But couldn't you keep them in the shade?" Steve asked. And then his face got red, as if he had said something rude. Peter could see that Steve had just remembered that the Bowmans had no real shade.

"Well, we're even," he thought. "We have no shade, they have no refrigerator."

"There's just a narrow strip behind the house," he said, "and they won't stay there. They want to crawl all around."

But just then Kate said, "We have lots of shade at our house."

Steve turned and scowled at her for mentioning it, but she went on in her timid voice: "I mean, if your mother would let you, couldn't you bring the twins to our house? They could play in the grass."

Jane and Peter both stared at her. That was a wonderful idea. There was all that good shade go-

ng to waste, and here were the twins having to be
kept in the house because it was too hot outdoors!

"Do you think your aunt would let us?" Jane
asked.

"I don't see why not," said Steve.

When Mother came in they asked her about it.
She looked doubtful.

"You'll have to ask Miss Jessup first," she said.
"It would be nice for the children, but we'll have to
be very sure your aunt won't mind."

They all went out in the garden then, and Steve
made several good suggestions. He knew a lot about
gardening.

"I think you should plant some portulaca or
something to cover up that bare ground until the
bigger plants come up," he said. "And I think you
need some fertilizer. This ground isn't much good.
It's cellar fill, mostly. There's hardly any topsoil."

"Why, Steve, how do you know?" Mother asked.

"I saw when they were building these houses,"
said Steve. "They took away most of the topsoil."

"You didn't like that, did you?" Mother asked.

"Well, would you?" Steve burst out suddenly.
"Taking down all the old houses and cutting down
the trees and digging up the gardens? If it hadn't

been for Aunt Matilda they would have done the same thing to Sea View."

Peter and Jane were astonished. Steve, who was so quiet, bursting out like that! They didn't know what to do. But Mother did.

"Let's sit down," she said, pulling Steve down beside her on the doorstep. "You must be very proud of Sea View," she went on. "Peter and Jane have been telling me about it. It must be lovely. I want to come and see it soon."

"Yes, ma'am," said Steve. "Aunt Matilda would like to have you." He looked a little ashamed of his outburst.

"I think a house like that is sort of like a museum," said Mother. "You want to keep things the way they've always been."

"That's what Aunt Matilda says," said Kate.

"And she is right," said Mother. "But what about the other houses? Were they beautiful too?"

"No," said Steve. "Some of them were falling down. The neighbors were glad to sell. They said Aunt Matilda was foolish to work so hard to keep an old place like ours. It's awful hard work."

"I know it is," said Mother. "But I think your aunt was right. She wanted to keep the house for you and Kate, because it's a good house. But the neighbors were right about their houses, because they didn't want them any more. And then," she added, "you have to think about us."

"About you?" Steve exclaimed.

"Yes. Where would we be if nobody built any little houses like this? Think of all the people who need houses!"

Steve grinned. He seemed to be feeling better. "I guess I didn't think of that," he said. "I just got mad when I saw all those little houses and all that cellar fill and those puny little trees."

"And that Mr. Krautkopf," said Kate. "He made you mad too."

Steve gave his sister a reproving look. Then he looked down at his shoes and said, "He's always trying to get Aunt Matilda to sell. He keeps telling her she could have a nice little house too, with a new kitchen. I—I guess it would be better for her. She wouldn't have to work so hard."

Peter remembered how Steve had stared at his mother's kitchen. Now he understood why.

Mother understood too. She patted his knee. "Some day," she said, "I just know your aunt will have a nice kitchen like mine. I think probably

107

you'll get it for her."

Steve flashed her a grateful look. She had said the right thing. "That's what I want to do," he said.

"And you will," said Mother. "But in the meantime, don't worry. I think your aunt is doing what she wants to do."

Steve stood up. "I—I guess we ought to get back," he said. "We've got all those beans to finish. Thanks for the lunch."

Mother walked to the gate with the children. "Come and see us again soon," she said.

CHAPTER 8

A Surprise for Aunt Matilda

They hurried off to Sea View, where they found Aunt Matilda cutting beans on the back porch. Kate and Jane sat down to help, and the boys picked up empty baskets and went out into the garden to pick more.

The hot afternoon sunshine poured down on their heads. Bees buzzed among the vines. Now and then a bird called.

Peter sat down on the ground, the better to reach the beans that hung down like green tassels among the thick green leaves. He picked with both hands.

"My, what a lot of string beans there are," he said. "When do you think we'll be through?"

"Oh, I guess in a couple of days," said Steve, picking on the other side of the row.

"That's good," said Peter. "Then we can do something else. You play ball?"

"The lima beans will be ripe then," said Steve.

"Lima beans!" said Peter.

"Sure, and after that the tomatoes."

"Help!" said Peter. "Don't you do anything all summer but can stuff?"

"We do quite a lot of it," Steve admitted. "Aunt Matilda says it's the only way we can manage."

Peter nodded. He understood now why Miss Jessup worked so hard. But at least, he thought, if she had a stove like Mother's it wouldn't be that hard.

Suddenly he sat up straight and threw a handful of beans into the basket.

"I just got an idea!" he exclaimed.

"I hope it's good," said Steve.

"It's swell. Why don't we buy your aunt a stove?
Surprise her!"

"Buy a stove?" said Steve. "Are you getting silly?
We haven't got enough money to buy a stove!"

"Well, not right now," said Peter, "but we could
earn some."

"How?" Steve demanded.

"Well, er—let's see." Peter hadn't thought about
that, but he couldn't let a little thing like that stop
him. "We could—maybe we could sell things."

"What things?"

"Oh, let's see," said Peter. "Have you got anything in your house that you don't need?"

"Sure, but Aunt Matilda wouldn't sell them."

Peter thought some more. Then he said, "Let's tell the girls. Jane sometimes has good ideas."

They seized the baskets, which were nearly full, and ran to the porch where the girls were waiting for them.

Looking to see that Aunt Matilda was out of earshot, Peter quickly told his idea. The girls listened carefully.

"Well, it's a good idea," said Jane, doubtfully.

"But how can we get the money?" Kate asked.

"How much have you got?" Steve asked her. "I have two dollars."

"I think I have about a dollar," said Kate.

"We have some," Peter began, but Steve stopped him.

"Oh, no," he said. "You can't give any."

Peter knew it would be no use insisting. The most Steve would let him do would be to help earn some. After all, they'd only known each other four days.

"We could mow people's lawns," he said.

"These people around here don't have any lawns," said Steve.

"We could make things to sell," Peter suggested. "For instance, I could make ship models."

"And I could write stories to sell," said Jane.

"I'd like to know," said Peter, "who'd be crazy enough to buy them."

"The same ones that would buy your ship models," Jane retorted. Her eyes flashed. She didn't like people to make fun of her writing.

"I think," Kate said, "that we ought to find out how much a stove costs."

"They can't be so terribly much," said Peter, "because ours came with the house. They wouldn't give them out free if they were very expensive."

"Well, let's go and ask Mr. Bunch," said Steve. "He'll tell us."

So as soon as the beans were finished, he asked Aunt Matilda if they could go down to the store for ice-cream cones.

Aunt Matilda said they could, and she came out with a shabby purse and gave Steve half a dollar.

"You treat the others," she said.

"Oh, no," Peter said. "We've got some money."

But Steve took the half dollar just the same and they started for the store.

It was a long hot walk down the dusty street. But at last they got to Mr. Bunch's store, and there in the middle of the floor was a beautiful white enamel stove like Mother's.

Mr. Bunch read the price tag on the stove

The four of them stood around and admired it. Pretty soon Mr. Bunch came over, mopping his bald head with a handkerchief.

"Well, ladies and gentlemen," he said, "it's warm for the time of year. What can I do for you? Anything in the hardware line, the dog line or the garden line?"

"We came to find out how much a stove costs," said Steve.

Mr. Bunch was flabbergasted. "A stove!" he exclaimed. "Isn't it hot enough for you as it is?"

"That's just it," said Peter. "It's too hot in his aunt's kitchen because she's just got that big coal stove. So we thought we'd buy her one that doesn't get so hot. How much is that one?"

Mr. Bunch stopped laughing and looked at them through the top part of his glasses. Then he raised his chin and looked at the tag on the stove through the lower part of the glasses.

"Well," he said, "it says here on this tag, two hundred dollars." And though he wasn't laughing, his eyes twinkled.

"Two hundred dollars!" they all said, in weak voices. Then they just stood and looked at each other. They could never get two hundred dollars!

"Oh, well, it was just an idea," said Peter.

"We really just came for some ice-cream cones," Steve explained, and they all started for the door.

"Now wait a minute," said Mr. Bunch.

They waited. Mr. Bunch said, "Wouldn't you like to look at something else, now that you're here?"

"No, thanks," said Steve, frowning. "We just had this idea, but of course it was silly. Sorry we bothered you."

"Now wait a minute," said Mr. Bunch. "It's no bother. I really meant it. You have the right idea. Your aunt does need a new stove. I can't think of anybody in Sea View Gardens who deserves it more. I've seen that big black monster she cooks on, and I think you're very smart children to think of her."

"Thanks," said Steve, still trying to get to the door. "But we haven't got two hundred dollars."

"How much have you got?" Mr. Bunch asked.

"Well, right now we have about three," said Steve. "Maybe we could earn some more——"

"Step right over here," said Mr. Bunch.

The four children followed him to the back of the store, wondering what he could be thinking of.

Lined up against the wall was an array of stoves.

They were smaller than the one in the middle of the floor, and each of them had a glass tank at one end, but they were all covered with the same gleaming white enamel.

"What you want," said Mr. Bunch, "is a *kerosene* stove. Of course those new-fangled electric ones are nice, but for real economy and convenience there's nothing like a good kerosene stove. Never could understand why Matilda Jessup didn't buy herself one. But you know how it is, we get attached to our things——"

"How—how much are they?" Peter asked.

"Well, now, young man," said Mr. Bunch, reading the tag on one that had three burners and a little top oven, "this one here is—let's see—you can have this for twenty dollars and fifty cents. How's that?"

And he turned to them with a broad smile on his face as if he had made a wonderful discovery.

The four children looked more cheerful. They all started to talk at once. Then they stopped.

Peter said, "Do you mind if we have a talk?"

"Not at all," said Mr. Bunch. "Take your time."

They put their heads together and whispered.

"If we could get him to keep it for us," said Peter, "maybe we could earn the rest of the money."

"We need seventeen dollars," said Steve.

"And fifty cents," said Jane.

"We could use the fifty cents Aunt Matilda gave us," Kate suggested.

"But if she asks us how the ice cream was?" said Steve.

"Oh, we'll say it was good," said Kate. "Ice cream is always good."

They giggled. Then Steve stepped up to Mr. Bunch and said, "We'd like to get Aunt Matilda a stove like that. Would you keep it till we get the rest of the money?"

"I'll be glad to," said Mr. Bunch. "And I'll tell you what I'll do. If you want to make a deposit of— say—three dollars, I'll give you a receipt, and then you'll know the stove is yours when you want it."

"That would be fine," said Steve. "Only, suppose we can't earn enough money, it wouldn't be fair, in case you want to sell the stove to somebody else."

"Well, you come around in a couple of weeks and let me know how you're making out," said Mr. Bunch. "I might get some ideas."

He went to a cluttered roll-top desk and, sitting down, wrote on a piece of paper:

July 19

Received of Mr. Stephen Jessup and Associates,
The sum of three dollars
As deposit on Stove No. 53218
To be held for payment in full of $20.50.
THEOPHILUS BUNCH, *Hardware.*

He handed this to Steve, and took the three dollars Steve gave him.

Kate pulled her brother's sleeve and whispered in his ear.

"She says," Steve announced, "that we should pay the extra fifty cents while we have it." And he held out Aunt Matilda's half dollar.

"All right," said Mr. Bunch. He changed the second line to read "three dollars and fifty cents," and put the money in his pocket.

"Now," he said, "I was just going next door to the drugstore to get a little liquid refreshment. This hot weather is awful for me. I keep on drinking soda and eating ice cream all the time. Would you people join me?"

"Oh, no, thanks," said Steve.

"We aren't thirsty," said Peter.

"We just had some water before we left," Jane explained.

"It would be a favor," said Mr. Bunch. "I get awfully lonesome."

So, leaving his assistant in charge, he led the four customers next door, where they sat on stools and ate ice cream and drank glasses of water.

Then they thanked Mr. Bunch and started home.

The way back seemed much shorter, for some reason. They talked about the stove they were going to get, and how much better it would be than an electric stove. For one thing, it didn't use electricity, and kerosene was much cheaper. And since

it was smaller, it wouldn't take up so much space in the kitchen.

All they had to do was earn seventeen dollars.

"That'll be our project," said Jane. "You know, we ought to have a name for it."

"What can we call it?" Kate asked.

"How about the Stove Club?"

Peter shook his head. "That's too ordinary."

"Well, what then?"

"What about Operation Stove?" said Peter.

"That's good," said Steve. "And we can call it O.S. when Aunt Matilda's around."

"Okay." Peter and Jane stopped at their gate and said good-by to their friends.

"See you tomorrow," said Peter.

"Tomorrow morning," Kate reminded him. "And don't forget the twins."

"We won't," said Jane. "And remember Operation Stove."

 # Operation Stove

Right after breakfast the next day, Peter and Jane piled the twins into their carriage, hitched up the Lieutenant on his leash, and hurried over to Sea View. Aunt Matilda had said it was all right to bring the babies. Kate and Steve were waiting for them, and they spread a blanket on the lawn and put the twins on it.

Then Aunt Matilda came out to greet them. She walked with her usual dignified step. But when she saw the babies, she sat right down on the grass and held out her arms, and Johnny, who had been examining a piece of grass, crawled right over and climbed into her lap. Then Peggy did the same, and Aunt Matilda sat there with her arms full of babies, looking perfectly happy.

"You sweet things!" she murmured.

Johnny reached up at her nose. She laughed.

123

"It's a long time since we had babies here," she said. Then she put them down and stood up and dusted the grass off her dress and said, "Well, there's much to be done," and went back into the house.

Steve said, "Well, I'll have to hoe the corn."

And Kate said, "I've got to make the beds." Jane and Peter were left to mind the babies.

Peter got out some of the toys they had brought along, a couple of dolls, and some cups and spoons and a ball. Jane got out her weaving. She was making a gaily colored pot-holder.

Peter had warned her that she wouldn't have much time to work on her pot-holder, because usually minding the twins meant getting up every minute to take some dirt out of Johnny's mouth or keep Peggy from crawling away out the gate.

But lo and behold! They were so contented on the blanket in the shade that they just sat quietly banging their spoons on their cups and never bothered their brother and sister at all. The Lieutenant curled up on a corner of the blanket and took a nap, and all was peace and quiet.

Pretty soon Kate came back.

"I finished my work," she said. "I came back to play with the babies." And she sat down and began to play peek-a-boo with Peggy.

A few minutes later Steve came along. He had decided to take a rest from hoeing. He sat down on the grass and began to roll the ball to Johnny. Johnny threw it back with loud chuckles of joy. He liked to play ball.

Not long after that Aunt Matilda came out again. She had a plate of cookies.

"I thought you children might like a snack," she said.

They were lemon cookies and she said the babies could have some too. They were very good.

The morning passed very quickly, and Jane was able to finish two pot-holders before it was time to take the babies home.

The next morning, Jane brought two little pot-holder looms. She showed Kate how to weave the yarn squares on it, and pretty soon they were both busily working.

When Aunt Matilda came in sight, the pot-holders were quickly pushed under a blanket.

"What are you going to do with all those pot-holders?" Steve asked.

"Operation Stove," Jane explained. "We thought

we'd see if we could sell them. Last year at school the girls made them to sell at the Fair. Lots of ladies need pot-holders."

"That's a good idea," said Steve. "I wish I could make something."

"Well, you really do," Jane said. "You've made that garden grow."

"Yes, but we can't sell any of it," said Steve. "We need all the vegetables for canning."

126

"What about the flowers?" Jane suggested. "You don't really need them."

"That's a good idea," said Kate. "Ladies like to buy flowers. You could pick bunches of them. We'll help you."

"And I have an idea what I can make," said Peter. "Remember, Jane, last year before I started making ship models I used to carve animals. I bet I could still do it."

"Sure you could," said Jane. "Dogs and cats. But I'm not sure what would be the best way to sell them. Should we go to people's houses?"

"I don't think Aunt Matilda would want us to," said Kate. "And I'd be scared anyhow."

Peter remembered something. "Mr. Bunch told us to come to him. Maybe he'd think of a way."

"Maybe he'd even sell them for us, the way he sold the puppies," Steve said.

So in the afternoon they walked to Mr. Bunch's store, carrying six pot-holders and three bunches of flowers.

Mr. Bunch was willing to help. He thought he could easily sell six pot-holders, and he put the flowers in a vase and set them in the window.

"It's good advertising," he said, when the chil-

127

dren thanked him. "It does me just as much good as you. The people stop and look, and then they come in, and usually they buy some hardware too."

Kate went home and rummaged in the yarn-bag for more colored wool, and Steve pulled weeds in the flower beds behind the chicken house, where Aunt Matilda seldom went.

Every day that week they worked—in the mornings while the twins played on the lawn, and in the afternoons when the twins were asleep. Peter carved cats and dogs. He tried to model the dogs after the Lieutenant, but the only way he could do that was to wait till the little dog was asleep. So Peter soon had a lot of little curled-up, sleeping dogs. Mr. Bunch said he could sell them all.

On Thursday, to the children's surprise, at about eleven o'clock in the morning, Mother appeared.

Peter and Jane jumped up and ran to meet her.

"Why, Mom," said Peter, "you're supposed to be writing your book. What are you doing here?"

"I came to see Miss Jessup," said Mother.

So they took her to the kitchen door. Aunt Matilda was washing clothes in a round tub set on two chairs. The kitchen was full of steam and the smell of soap and hot water.

Aunt Matilda dried her hands on her apron and came out on the back porch.

"How do you do, Mrs. Bowman," she said. "I'm glad to meet you. It has been so nice having your children here."

"I felt I should come and see that my children were not in the way," said Mother. "They're very helpful at home, and I hope they try to help elsewhere too."

Aunt Matilda smiled. "I feel they're part of our home too," she said. "We've grown very fond of your children."

129

Then Mother and Aunt Matilda exchanged one of those grown-up looks that meant that they liked each other, and liked each other's families, and were going to get along fine.

"This is a beautiful house," said Mother, looking around.

"I believe it is one of the best houses of its kind," said Aunt Matilda.

Then she took Mother on a tour of the house while the children went back to the babies.

At lunch that day Mother kept talking about how beautiful the house was, and how nice Aunt Matilda was, until even Peter and Jane got a little tired of it.

"But what a shame it is that she can't afford a few modern improvements," said Mother. "She had to work so hard. Why, she's still washing clothes the way they did sixty years ago. But I'm sure she wouldn't allow anyone to help her."

Then Peter decided it was time to tell Mother about Operation Stove, and she thought it was a fine idea too.

She promised to buy several pot-holders and as many flowers as Steve could spare. She offered to lend them the money so that they could buy the stove at once and then pay her back later, but Peter was sure that Steve wouldn't allow that.

"I guess not," said his mother. "He's proud, just like his aunt."

"I guess we'll have to save up until we get enough," said Peter.

By the end of the first week, they had earned three dollars and twenty cents.

"I wish we could go faster," Jane complained. "It's the 26th of July already. By the time we get enough the summer will be gone and all the canning done and Aunt Matilda won't have the good of it."

And then something happened. One day when they were pushing the twins off to Sea View in their carriage, Mrs. MacDermott called to them from her yard.

"Where in the world do you go every day with those babies?" she asked.

Jane explained about Sea View.

"And what is Miss Jessup like?" Mrs. MacDermott asked. "Is she really stand-offish?"

Then Jane had to explain that Aunt Matilda was very nice, and so were Steve and Kate.

"Do you think," said Mrs. MacDermott, "that you could take Teddy and Joany with you a couple of times this week? I have to paint my living room and they'd get right in the paint. I was going to ask if they could play in your yard, but then I noticed you went away every morning. I'd be willing to pay of course."

This was a new idea with great possibilities. Peter and Jane gave each other a quick look and said hastily that they'd have to find out and let Mrs. MacDermott know.

They hurried to Sea View and told Steve and Kate. Then they all rushed to Aunt Matilda.

"Would you mind," they asked, all talking at once, "if we brought the MacDermott children over to play in the yard too? They're awfully nice children. Teddy is three and Joany is two. They live next door, and it's so hot in their yard."

Aunt Matilda looked doubtful. "The trouble is," she said, "that if we let these two come, we ought to let others come too."

"Oh, but of course we couldn't invite *every body*," Jane exclaimed. "There wouldn't be room."

"Well, all right, then," said Aunt Matilda.

So Jane rushed back and told Mrs. MacDermott who came right over with the children.

Mrs. MacDermott admired the house and liked Aunt Matilda just as much as Mother had liked her.

oany and Teddy were happily playing with the Lieutenant on the grass, and when she asked whether they would mind if she went home for a while, they just said, "Good-by, Mommy!"

So off she went. Pretty soon Aunt Matilda came out on the lawn with a glass jar in her hand. It contained peppermint sticks, and she handed them out to everybody except the twins, who were chewing zwieback.

"My mother always kept peppermint sticks for children who came visiting," she said, "and I just remembered I had these."

Then she sat down and read the MacDermott children a story out of an old picture book she had brought out.

Mrs. MacDermott came back in an hour, because she thought that would be long enough for the first time, but the children were so contented, they didn't even notice her. And when she took them away they cried.

"Go back to trees!" they wailed as their mother urged them down the street.

"Yes, tomorrow you will go back," she promised.

The next morning Jane collected them and she and Peter started out with four babies for Sea View.

Mrs. MacDermott had said she would pay them twenty-five cents a day for each child. Operation Stove was progressing beautifully, and the shady lawn under the big trees was a busy place.

Then the next day Mrs. MacDermott said that her friend Mrs. Carter wondered if they could take her little boy Oscar. Oscar was three, and he was Teddy's special friend, and Mrs. Carter had walked past Sea View and thought it marvelous.

The children asked Aunt Matilda about it that

morning, and at first she shook her head and said they would have to draw the line somewhere. But then Mrs. Carter came by with her friend Mrs. MacDermott to get Teddy and Joany, and she had Oscar with her, and when Aunt Matilda saw Oscar, she just melted.

It was not surprising, because three-year-old Oscar was such a nice little boy. He had broad shoulders and a deep voice and a crew haircut, and the kind of grin that nobody could resist. But it just

135

seemed that Aunt Matilda couldn't resist any kind of baby.

"All right," she said. "Oscar may come, but no more."

And the next day she brought out some very old blocks made of smooth stone for the children to play with, and the day after that, when the grass was damp because it had rained in the night, she brought out an old wooden train and a doll house and let the children play on the front porch.

She helped Peter and Steve hang a swing from the lowest branch of the sycamore tree, and she found some big cardboard boxes for the babies to climb in and out of. She seemed to be having fun.

People began coming by and looking in through the fence. At first they just seemed curious, and then Mrs. MacDermott said that if Aunt Matilda wanted to, she could have any number of children. But of course Jane and Peter had to say no, they couldn't take any more.

Minding the twins had just been a matter of sitting around and being ready to jump when one of them ate some grass or pulled the other's hair. But looking after five children was *work*. Peter and Steve especially found it very tiring, and went off now and then to rest up by hoeing in the garden or cleaning out the chicken house, until the girls accused them of shirking.

After that they took Teddy and Joany and Oscar with them and let them dig in the soft earth, or scatter corn to the chickens. The hens soon got to know the younger children and came running as soon as they appeared.

"Here, chicken, chicken," Oscar would call.

"Eat up your dinner," Teddy would tell them.

Joany didn't talk much. She just waved her arms and squealed.

One day there was a surprise at the chicken house. Abigail was not sitting on her nest. Instead she was walking around importantly, surrounded by a family of ten downy chicks.

"Peep! Peep!" the chicks cried, running after her.

The youngsters squeaked with joy and tried to catch the fluffy little live balls. But Abigail clucked to them and led them off to the other end of the chicken yard.

Steve was very proud. "That's a good hen," he said. "She'll take good care of those chicks." And he gave Abigail an extra helping of corn.

They herded the three youngsters back to the lawn, and stayed there while Kate and Jane went to look at the new chicks.

Oscar climbed on Steve as though he were a mountain, and Joany tried to eat Peter's ear while the Lieutenant took a bite of Peggy's zwieback.

Peter laughed. "I never thought I'd be spending my vacation baby-sitting," he said.

But later, when they counted up their money and looked at the calendar that hung beside the big black stove, they knew it was worth while. In another week they would have enough money for the stove. It was a wonderful feeling.

CHAPTER 10

A Letter

At last it was the Monday they had been waiting for. Lunch was over, the twins were napping, and Peter and Jane were ready to go downtown. They looked very snappy in new dungarees and polo shirts. Jane's black hair was neatly brushed. Peter's crew cut stood on end like a very short scrubbing-brush. He had had a brand-new haircut on Saturday. You had to be slicked up for an occasion like this. It wasn't every day one went downtown and bought a stove.

Operation Stove had been a success. They had enough money, and all they had to do was go and get Steve and Kate, and then proceed to Mr. Bunch's store.

They had to hurry. They were a little late because they had waited for the postman, and there had been a letter from Father.

139

They had written to him about Operation Stove and he approved of it heartily. He said he was glad they were becoming useful members of the community, and to go right ahead with more projects when that one was finished.

It was nice to think of themselves as useful members of the community. Now that they came to think of it, that *was* what they were. The babies they took care of were helped by the shade and coolness of Sea View. The mothers were getting some free time, Sea View was getting a stove, Aunt Matilda was getting acquainted with some neighbors—which she wouldn't have done otherwise—and Mr. Bunch would be able to sell the stove and make a profit. Operation Stove was quite a big thing.

So, with praise from their superior officer making them feel proud and important, they set out for Sea View. As they arrived, they could see that the postman had been there too, and was just going away.

"Well," said Peter, "I hope he's left them a nice letter like ours."

As they came up the gravel path, they could see that he had left a letter. But it wasn't a nice one. Aunt Matilda was standing on the top step with the letter in her hand, and Steve and Kate were standing on either side of her, looking as scared as if they had seen a ghost. Aunt Matilda's face was white.

Peter and Jane stood still, wishing they knew what was the matter, but afraid to come up if they weren't wanted.

Finally Jane broke the silence. "What's wrong?" she asked. "Has anything happened?"

Aunt Matilda looked at her in a puzzled way, and said, "Nothing you could help, my dear."

"Oh, but what is it? Maybe we *can* help," Jane persisted.

Peter gave her a nudge to tell her to keep still, but Jane wouldn't pay any attention to him. "Please, Aunt Matilda," she repeated.

Aunt Matilda sat down in her rocking chair and looked down at the letter in her lap. Kate looked more and more scared, and then she began to cry.

Aunt Matilda took her in her lap and rocked her. "Don't cry, child," she said. "I'm sure everything will be all right. I was just surprised. But now I must think what to do."

"But couldn't you just tell us?" Jane asked again. "We won't say anything to anybody."

"Let's tell them," said Steve. "They're our friends."

"All right," said Aunt Matilda. "But children, there's nothing you can do about it, so please don't let it worry you. It's a letter from the city."

"Is it taxes?" Steve asked.

"No," said Aunt Matilda. "Taxes are bad enough. But this letter says that our house has some things the matter with it that have to be fixed. You see, we don't have the right kind of pipes."

"You mean the well?" said Steve.

"Yes, partly," said Aunt Matilda. "It didn't matter when there were just a few houses around here, but now there are so many, they all have to have the right kind of water supply. And we don't."

"Could you have them fixed?" Peter asked.

"Yes, we could, but it would cost a great deal of money," said Aunt Matilda. "And there are some more things. We aren't supposed to keep goats or chickens."

"You could sell them," said Jane.

"But then," said Steve, "we'd have to buy eggs and milk."

"Yes, that's right," said Jane. "I forgot. Then what can you do?"

"We may have to sell the house," said Aunt Matilda, sadly.

142

Aunt Matilda took Kate on her lap

Jane jumped. "Sell the house!" she squeaked. "You can't! Why, we were just——"

Peter gave her a poke and she kept quiet.

"I know," said Aunt Matilda. "You were just getting acquainted and having so much fun."

Kate had stopped crying. She dried her face with her hands. She and Steve looked at each other. They understood that what their aunt had been trying to prevent might happen after all.

"Mr. Krautkopf has been asking me to sell it," Aunt Matilda continued. "I think he will give me a good price."

Jane got very angry. "It's all that Mr. Krautkopf's fault!" she exclaimed. "I bet he's the one that went and told the city about the pipes and the chickens! I just bet he is!"

"Now, you mustn't say that," said Aunt Matilda. "If it's wrong to have them, we can't help it."

Jane was very quiet for a while. Then she said, "I know what you could do, Aunt Matilda. You could be a benefit to the community like Daddy said. You could get lots of ladies to come and leave their babies here, and we could all mind them and have a real nursery school, and they would all pay you lots of money——"

144

She suddenly realized that she had given away part of the secret. She clapped her hand over her mouth. Peter, Kate and Steve looked horrified.

Aunt Matilda looked startled too.

"Children!" she said. "Do you mean you have been accepting *money* for looking after the babies?"

"Well," they all began, and then stopped. It was very embarrassing. Peter felt like giving Jane a good shake.

He spoke up. "It was in a good cause," he said, "and it wasn't very *much* money. And the ladies were *glad* to have us do it."

"Oh, I know they were," said Aunt Matilda. "But, child, we can't accept money for helping our neighbors."

"We didn't know you wouldn't like it, Aunt Matilda," said Steve, "and the kids had an awfully good time here."

"I know they did," said Aunt Matilda. "And I enjoyed having them. It's true there is no park or any shady place for them in the neighborhood. If Mr. Krautkopf were going to make a park of Sea View, perhaps I might not feel so badly, but I think he's going to build a supermarket."

"A supermarket!" said all four children, indignantly. "He *can't* do that!"

"Well, if he buys it, of course he can," said Aunt Matilda. "But now I can't sit here any more. I must go to town and see whoever is in charge of these things. I will go and dress now, and perhaps I can catch the two o'clock train." And she set Kate down and went upstairs.

The four children sat on the top step with their chins in their hands. There was no use in going for the stove now. It almost seemed that there was no use in anything.

From the shed came the sleepy clucking of the hens. Pretty soon they would be gone. They would be laying eggs for somebody else, or even worse, they would be sold to a butcher shop and somebody would make soup out of them. And what would happen to Taffy? And the little chicks? And what about all the lovely things in the house?

After a while Aunt Matilda came out, dressed for town. She looked strange in a suit and a hat and gloves. The children were used to seeing her in a blue gingham dress and a white apron.

"I shall try to be back in time for supper," she said. "You children do the chores and set the table."

"Couldn't they come to our house for supper?"

146

Jane said. "I'm sure Mother wouldn't mind."

"I wouldn't like to inconvenience her," said Aunt Matilda. But you could see she was willing.

"It wouldn't," said Jane. "We're only having beans for supper and Mother can always open another can."

"All right," said Aunt Matilda, smiling. "I'll come for you there. But Stephen and Kate, take along a bag of the molasses cookies. And you may each have one now." And she kissed Kate and patted Steve and went away down the street. The children listened to her footsteps getting fainter.

After a while, Steve said, "Shucks!"

Peter said, "There's no use sitting here. We ought to do something."

"What can we do?" Steve asked.

Jane made a contribution. "I know," she said. "You remember Mother said this place was like a museum. We could put up a sign and have people come to see it and charge admission."

"It's an idea," said Peter.

But Steve shook his head. "Aunt Matilda wouldn't like it," he said.

"Well, then," said Jane, who seemed to be full of ideas, "we could print a lot of sheets of paper saying that this house is a famous old house and ought not to be torn down. A sort of petition. And pass them around for people to sign. I heard of some people who did that once."

"No, Aunt Matilda wouldn't like it," said Steve.

Then Jane got mad. "It seems to me your aunt doesn't like anything," she said, her eyes flashing.

"You've got some nerve saying that," Steve retorted.

"Well, she's right!" Peter shouted. "Everything we say to try to help you, you object to!"

"Who asked you to help anyhow?" Steve yelled.

Kate added, "Yes, we don't need your help!"

And then they were all yelling at each other, and the girls both began to cry, and suddenly all four stopped and looked at each other, ashamed.

Steve was the first to speak. "I'm sorry I said that," he said. "I don't know why I said it."

"It was our fault," said Peter, feeling very foolish. "We shouldn't have said that about helping you. Of course you don't need us to help you."

"Well, we do," said Steve. "Anybody could see that we need some kind of help, but what can we do? Aunt Matilda needs a whole lot of money and how can we get it?"

148

Jane got that faraway look in her eyes that came from reading too many library books.

"If only we could discover a long-lost treasure," she sighed, "the way they do in books, when the family's failing fortunes have to be restored!"

They all laughed at that, and then they felt better, and Kate went inside and got the molasses cookies, and they sat on the top step and ate them. Jane told the story of the last book she had read, in which the heroine discovered a secret room in an old house, where all the family jewels had been hidden when the family ran away from the Indians.

Then Kate giggled and said, "Well, we could look for great-grandmother's rings."

And Jane sat up straight and said, "Of course! Why didn't we think of it sooner?"

"Why, what use would it be?" Steve asked.

"Well, if we could find them," said Jane, "wouldn't that be a help?"

"Of course," said Steve. "But we could never find them. Why, everybody looked all over the place for them, and asked everybody that was here. They just aren't in the house, that's all. Gosh, if anybody could have found them they certainly could have used them long ago, just as much as now."

Peter and Jane sat up straight on the step and asked, "What do you mean?"

"Well, didn't Aunt Matilda tell you about great-grandfather's ship?"

"You mean the *Flying Swallow?* No. What about her? She just said your great-grandmother went up in the tower and saw the ship in the harbor, and then the rings were lost, and the next thing your great-grandfather came in his carriage, and he liked the picture."

"Well, that isn't the end of the story," said Steve. "About the first thing he said to his wife was, 'Where are the rings?' He needed them, because the ship had been in a terrible storm and was all banged up, and they had lost all the cargo, and he needed to sell the rings to get money to have the ship fixed and pay for the cargo. And of course the rings were lost."

"So what happened?" Peter asked breathlessly.

"So they couldn't find the rings," said Steve. "So he lost the ship."

"And did he get another?"

"No. He could never get another. He got a job as a captain on somebody else's ship, but it wasn't the same as his own."

"Oh!" said Peter. This was a very sad ending to a story. He could hardly bear to think of the beautiful *Flying Swallow* all battered from the storm, and then sold because Captain Jessup couldn't have her fixed up.

And now the same thing was going to happen to his house. It was too much. It made him angry.

"It just isn't fair!" he exclaimed, banging his fist on the step.

But Jane was thinking. "I don't think anybody stole them," she said. "I think they're here."

"Then why haven't we found them?" Steve asked.

"Because it's a mystery," said Jane. "We have to

151

unravel it. Now if only we knew where that secret drawer was!"

"Oh, that's easy," said Steve. "It's up in Aunt Matilda's room. I could show it to you."

"Oh!" said Jane. She sounded disappointed. "I thought you didn't know where it was!"

"Oh, of course we know," said Steve. "Great-grandmother had to show it to the family when they were looking for the rings. Only there's nothing in it."

"Could we see it?" Jane asked.

Steve and Kate consulted. "Do you think Aunt Matilda would mind?" Kate asked.

"We wouldn't hurt anything," said Steve. "Let's show them."

CHAPTER 11

More Marbles, a Thimble and a Spool of Thread

They went upstairs. The house seemed very big and empty with no grownup in it. It was so quiet that Peter found himself walking on tiptoe. And Steve felt the same way, for when he pushed open Aunt Matilda's door, he whispered, "It's in here."

Peter and Jane had not often been upstairs. They had been in Steve's room, which had once been his grandfather's, and in Kate's, which had been Aunt Matilda's when she was little. But they had never seen this room, which used to belong to Aunt Matilda's mother.

There was a high four-poster bed, and near the window there was an odd-looking chest. It was made of light brown wood, and along each edge there was a strip of ebony. The knobs on the drawers were little ebony balls.

153

Steve pushed one of the balls, and at the same time he pushed somewhere along the strip that ran up and down the edge, and all at once a little drawer sprang right out of the front of the big drawer. There were some handkerchiefs in the little drawer.

"Well, for goodness' sake!" said Jane. "Isn't that cute! Are you sure there's nothing but handkerchiefs in there?"

"Of course," said Steve. And he pushed the drawer shut. When it was shut you couldn't see where it had been. The grain of the wood matched perfectly and there wasn't even a line to show the edge of the little drawer.

"Wait," said Peter, "open it again. I heard something rattle."

"Oh, that!" said Steve. And he pushed the ball and the ebony strip. Sure enough, as the little drawer sprang out there was a rattle. It wasn't loud, because of the handkerchiefs.

"What was that?" Peter demanded.

"Oh, that's a marble," said Steve.

"A marble! What's it doing there?"

Steve laughed. "I don't know," he said. "It's always been there. I guess to fool people. I bet you thought the rings were in there."

All at once the secret drawer sprang out

Peter wouldn't admit that. "Well, of course I didn't think so," he said. "But it kind of got me excited for a minute."

"I guess I thought the same thing the first time I saw it," said Steve. "When Aunt Matilda first told us the story and showed us the drawer, it rattled just like that, and she laughed."

"Did your aunt put it there?" Peter demanded.

"No," said Steve. "She said it was always in there, and she just never took it out."

"Well, look," said Jane, "if your grandfather, that is, Aunt Matilda's brother, put the marble in, it means he must have known where the secret drawer was. Maybe he took the rings out."

Steve and Kate both looked shocked. "Oh, Grandfather wouldn't have done a thing like that!" said Kate.

"Maybe he did it for a joke," Jane persisted, "and then couldn't remember where he had put them."

"Oh, no!" Steve insisted. "Why, his father lost his ship because they couldn't find the rings. He wouldn't have done that!"

Peter and Jane could see the sense of that, of course. Jane walked to the window and looked out.

"Look," she said, "there's the sycamore right outside this window! I bet you could climb right out onto it."

The others came and stood beside her. The big tree seemed near enough to jump to, but Steve shook his head.

"It looks that way, but you really couldn't," he said. "I bet you were thinking that somebody stole the rings and then climbed down the tree and ran away with them. But I don't think so. He'd make quite a lot of noise jumping and he'd probably fall down and break his leg."

"Well, I bet," said Jane, "that somebody could sit in the tree and see where the secret drawer was when your great-grandmother opened it."

Steve looked startled. "You've got an idea there," he said. "I didn't think of that before."

"Well, suppose somebody did that," said Peter. "He'd know where the rings were, and then he'd come and steal them when nobody was looking. But what good is it?"

"What do you mean what good is it?" Jane asked.

"The rings wouldn't be here," said Peter.

"Oh, that's right," said Jane.

She walked away from the window. "Where does this door go to?" she asked, turning a knob.

157

"Oh, that goes to my room," said Steve. He pushed the door open so that she could look in. "It used to be my grandfather's."

"Yes, I know," said Jane. She pulled the door shut again, and they all walked out into the hall.

What were they to do now? The secret drawer wasn't a secret any more, and there was nothing in it but some handkerchiefs and a marble. Steve was

starting down the stairs when Peter stopped him.

"Could we go up in the cupola again?" he asked.

"Well, I guess so," said Steve. "There's nothing else to do." And instead of going down they went up.

Steve opened the windows to let the fresh air in, and they stood and looked down over the treetops and the houses that looked like a toy village, and the harbor, far away, with its toy boats.

Peter tried to imagine that he could see the *Flying Swallow* out there on the water, with all sails spread, the men hauling on the ropes or climbing in the rigging, singing sailors' chanteys as they worked.

But the *Flying Swallow* was gone. All that was left was the little ship model down on the mantelpiece in the parlor. And pretty soon that would be gone too. It made him feel sad. He looked around for something to do.

There was a seat running all around the little room under the windows. Peter climbed up on it and put his hand on the top of the window frame to hold on by. There was a groove behind the frame and as his fingers sank into the fluffy dust that lay there, he felt something hard and round. He pulled his hand out in a hurry.

"What's the matter?" Steve asked.

"There's something in there!" said Peter.

"What is it?" Jane cried. "Quick, get it out!"

"I don't know," said Peter. "There's all that dust, and it's too high to see." He was standing on tiptoe.

Steve said to Kate, "Go down and get the little footstool from Aunt Matilda's room."

Kate ran. In a minute she was back with the stool. Steve put it on the window seat and Peter

160

stood on it and looked into the crack. The first thing he did was to sneeze.

Steve said, "Kate, go down and get a dust rag to wipe up that dust." But Peter stopped her.

"I have a handkerchief," he said.

He brushed out the worst of the dust.

"What is it? What is it?" the others demanded.

Peter pulled out the thing he had felt. It was a spool of thread!

"Oh, shucks!" said Steve.

"That's what I say," said Peter. "What good is a spool of thread? What sense does it make?"

It didn't make any sense at all. They all stood there looking at the spool of thread.

But at last Jane said, "Well, don't stop. Go on. See if there's anything else there."

Peter dusted around some more and felt in the crack. A little farther on he felt something else. He pulled the thing out. It was a very small thimble.

"It looks as if your great-grandmother kept her sewing things in here," he said, handing it to Kate.

But Kate rubbed it on her dungarees and looked at it closely. "It's not great-grandmother's," she said. "It's got an M on it. I wonder if it could be Aunt Matilda's."

"She never said anything about losing a thim ble," said Steve.

"Well, why should she?" Peter asked. He couldn' see why anyone should want a thimble anyway.

But now they were all getting excited.

"See if there's anything else in there!" Jan shouted.

"Let me look," said Steve. "I'm taller."

"No, I'll look," said Peter.

But Steve ran down to the floor below and cam up with a couple of boxes and he and Jane climbe up and started poking dust out with their handker chiefs, and poor little Kate jumped up and down yelling, "Let me see, let me see!"

They stirred up an awful lot of dust, but foun nothing for quite a while, until suddenly Stev yelled, "I've got something!"

And he held out a fistful of dust and in the mid dle of it was—another marble!

They all looked at it in disgust. After all that ex citement, to find nothing but a marble!

"Your grandfather sure did scatter marble around," said Peter. "What was the idea, anyhow?

Steve shook his head. It didn't make sense at al

"And what about the other things?" Peter aske

162

"Maybe he put the hair bow in the tree to tease your aunt, but why should he put a spool of thread in this crack?"

"He might have been teasing Aunt Matilda," said Kate. "She might have been sewing and he might have hidden her thread and her thimble."

"Well, yes," said Peter. But he wasn't satisfied. Something was bothering him. Finally he figured out what it was.

"Wouldn't you think," he said, "that when every-body was hunting for the rings, they would have found some of these marbles and things, and taken them out?"

It did seem so, unless—unless what?

"Well," said Jane, "unless the marbles were put there after they stopped looking for the rings, or unless they didn't look in the places where we've been finding the marbles."

"But they must have looked in the secret drawer," said Steve, "and there's a marble in there."

"Well, your grandfather must have put that in there afterward, then," said Peter.

"And you're sure," said Jane, "that he couldn't have taken the rings out to tease his mother? You said he was such a tease."

But Steve and Kate just wouldn't believe that that was possible.

"You know his room was right next to his mother's," Jane went on. "He might have peeked through the door when she was opening the drawer."

"Yes, or he might have climbed the sycamore and peeked," said Steve. "And maybe he lost the marble in the tree, and hid the bow there, but he wouldn't take those rings."

164

He closed the windows, and they went slowly down the stairs. It was time to do the chores. The late afternoon sunlight slanted through the quiet house, and out in the shed the chickens were calling for their supper.

The four children fed them and collected the eggs, milked Taffy the goat and put the milk and eggs in the cellar.

Then they set out for the Bowmans' house.

CHAPTER 12

What Fell Out of the Cradle

It was late when Aunt Matilda came back. The supper dishes had been washed and put away, and the twins had long since been put to bed, and Mother and the four children were playing cassino in the living room, when they heard her footsteps coming up the walk.

Aunt Matilda was quite tired from her trip to town. She wasn't used to riding on trains and walking on city streets and finding her way around office buildings.

"I'd rather do a week's wash," she said, taking the chair Mother offered her.

The children crowded around her, asking questions.

"Children, let Miss Jessup rest," Mother said.

But Aunt Matilda shook her head. "They want to know, and they might just as well know."

166

The news she brought was not good. It was just as the letter had said—the new pipes would have to be put in, and as she couldn't do that, Sea View would have to be sold.

But Aunt Matilda was cheerful. She wasn't going to have any more crying.

She looked around the living room and said, "This is a nice little house. Perhaps Mr. Kraut-kopf is right. He says we would do much better in one of these than at Sea View."

"That Mr. Krautkopf!" said Steve hotly.

"Now, Stephen," said Aunt Matilda, "think how much less work there would be for me in a little house like this. It's only common sense. And now, we must be going."

"Oh, not yet," said Mother. "You must have some supper first."

Aunt Matilda consented to have a cup of tea, and while the water was boiling she inspected the rest of the house. She peeped in at the sleeping twins, and smiled.

"It was so nice having your babies for a little while," she said to Mother. "If only I had thought of it sooner!"

"The babies loved it," said Mother.

"And we were being a benefit to the community, as Peter says," said Aunt Matilda.

Peter felt his face getting red, but by good luck nobody noticed.

Then Aunt Matilda looked about the kitchen.

"This is really a very fine kitchen," she said. "Not a bit like mine. But one would have to run all this machinery. However, it might not be difficult."

She drank her cup of tea and then stood up.

"Come, Stephen and Kate," she said, "we must go. And Peter and Jane, if you would like to come to Sea View tomorrow, I shall have something for each of you."

When they had gone, Peter said, "Isn't it funny, Aunt Matilda almost seems glad she's going to sell Sea View."

"I don't think she's glad," Mother said. "She's probably relieved to have the matter settled. And she's brave. It's not easy to start a new way of living at her age."

Peter nodded. It was all true but he didn't like it. He wished there were more time for them to hunt for the missing rings. He wished it could all wait till Dad came back. But Dad would not be back till sometime in September and now it was barely the middle of August. Well, they would just keep looking as long as they could, though it was very much like looking for a needle in a haystack, as grownups liked to say.

"I guess we might as well leave the pup home today," he told Jane the next afternoon as they started out for Sea View. "We'll be too busy to take care of him and he'll get into mischief."

The Lieutenant had lately taken to running out and barking when anyone went past. He was also apt to chew things if nobody paid attention to him.

"Okay," said Jane. She went back and shut him up in her room.

But they had not gone far when there was a loud yapping and a scratching of nails on the pavement. There was the little black dog coming after them.

"How did you get out?" Jane demanded.

"Go back!" Peter shouted.

But the Lieutenant obviously believed that every time they went to Sea View he had to come along. Tongue hanging out, tail wagging, he stood and waited to be picked up.

"You're getting awfully spoiled," said Peter, hoisting him up in his arms. "And heavy too. There's no reason why you can't walk."

The Lieutenant reached up and gave Peter's face a lick.

"That's all right," said Peter, sternly. "Just behave yourself when we get there. And don't bother Aunt Matilda. She has enough trouble without you."

But when they arrived, Aunt Matilda didn't look troubled. She had made up her mind, and she was not going to waste time in regrets. She had a cloth around her hair, and a big apron over her dress.

"Today," she said, "I am going to start cleaning the attic. You children may help me if you like."

And she started up the stairs. The four children held a conference.

"Let's keep our eyes open," Jane whispered. "Maybe we can still find the rings."

"Okay," Steve whispered back, "but I doubt it."

"Well, it doesn't hurt to look," said Peter.

They went up to the third floor and Aunt Matilda opened one of the doors. It was dark in the attic. There was only a small window at the end. Queer shapes loomed up all around, looking like black ghosts in the twilight until Aunt Matilda turned on the light.

Then they saw what the queer shapes were. There was a bird cage on top of a trunk, and a globe and a dressmaker's dummy and an artist's easel. There was a suit of armor and a lot of old guns and some chests of drawers and some more trunks, and on one of the chests stood a large stuffed rooster.

Aunt Matilda went to one of the trunks.

"There are a lot of letters in here," she said, "and I'm going to look through them for a little while. You children may look around and see if you find anything that interests you."

Peter squeezed past the trunks to get a look at the guns that hung on a rack on the wall.

Kate opened a trunk, and Peter heard Jane exclaim, "Oh! How beautiful!"

He looked, and she was lifting a doll out of the trunk. And then Kate lifted out another one.

"Oh, you've found my old dolls," said Aunt Matilda.

"Can we play with them?" Kate asked.

"You may each take something from here," said Aunt Matilda. "We shall have to send away most of the things in the house, but each of us will take something he or she likes very much."

"Could I have this doll, then?" Kate asked.

Aunt Matilda took the doll in her arms and smoothed its blue satin dress and its black hair. She

172

lifted the dress and looked at the embroidered petticoats and the tiny kid shoes.

"This is Evelina," she said. "And the other is her sister, Louisa. Mother made their clothes. Yes, you may have her if you like."

"And could I have the other?" Jane asked.

"Yes," said Aunt Matilda, "and their clothes are in that trunk too, I think."

The girls went back to the trunk to get the clothes.

Steve lifted down the rooster. "I'd like to have this," he said.

Aunt Matilda laughed. "You want that? That's Josephus, my father's prize rooster. He could crow louder than any other rooster in the county. My mother was glad when he passed on, but Father was so sad he had him stuffed."

"I want him to remind me of our chickens," said Steve.

"All right," said Aunt Matilda. "And Peter, what would you like?"

But Peter shook his head. "I don't know yet," he said. "Could I think about it?"

"Of course," said Aunt Matilda.

Then Jane cried, "Oh, *look* at the darling cradle!"

Kate said, "That was great-grandfather's cradle, wasn't it, Aunt Matilda? Could we take it to put the dolls in?"

Aunt Matilda nodded. "Yes, of course. I used to rock them in that cradle. And Thomas and I used to put the monkey to bed in it." She bent over her trunkful of old letters once more.

"Come on, Steve," said Kate. "Help us carry these things downstairs."

Steve took the cradle and the girls each carried a doll and an armful of dolls' clothes, while Peter lugged the rooster on its stand. It was heavy. Its shiny glass eye glared at him, as if it were startled to find itself moving after so many years.

"Don't drop that," Steve directed. "That's a valuable rooster. I bet it's a museum piece. I bet it's the most valuable thing in the whole house."

Peter didn't think so. He thought there were much better things in the house—the ship's clock, for instance, or the picture over the mantel in the parlor, or the *Flying Swallow*. But he didn't say so.

They took the things out under the sycamore tree where it was cooler, and set them down on the grass.

With a joyful bark, the Lieutenant came racing around the corner of the house. He had been lonesome on the porch with nobody but his mother for company.

"Yap! Yap!" he barked. Then he stopped still. He walked up to the cradle and sniffed it. Then he growled. The hair on his back stood up. He seized the blankets in his teeth and gave them a shake.

"Stop that!" Jane cried, reaching out to pull him away. Then she squealed, "Oh!"

A small mouse had jumped out of the cradle and was running across the grass. The Lieutenant galloped after it, but it dashed under the porch. He squatted down to wait for it, growling fiercely.

"He's hunting," said Steve.

"I guess he sniffed it among the blankets," said Kate. "Ow! There's some more!" She had lifted a little blanket out of the cradle and it had come apart. The mice had chewed holes in it, and now two more little mice jumped out and ran away.

"I guess they were babies," said Jane. "I wonder where their mother is. Maybe she's at home looking all over and wondering what has become of her children."

"Well, we can't help it," said Kate. "Let's clean this old cradle out." And she pulled everything out —mattress, blankets and pillow, and tossed the things on the grass.

Then she dumped the whole thing over in order to toss out the mouse nest, when something fell to the ground with a soft thud and a rattle.

"What was that?" Jane asked.

"I don't know," said Kate, searching in the grass.

"It was this," said Jane, holding out something.

In her hand she held a small leather bag. She shook it and it rattled.

"Open it," said Peter. "Hurry up, what are you waiting for?"

Steve's face was pale. He couldn't say a word.

Jane's fingers fumbled with the dried-up old drawstring. At last it broke, and out spilled—more marbles!

At this the four of them just sat back and laughed. Peter was so exasperated he could have cried. Anyway he could have said a few words he wasn't supposed to say.

"They ought to change the name of this house," Jane exclaimed. "Call it Marble Mansion instead of Sea View."

"Did your great-grandfather take marbles to bed with him when he was a baby?" Peter asked.

"I never heard of it," said Steve.

"I bet I know who did," said Kate softly.

The other three turned on her. "Yes? Who did it? Tell us, if you're so smart."

"It was the monkey," said Kate.

Steve stared at her in amazement. "How do you know?" he asked.

"Well, didn't you hear Aunt Matilda say they used to rock the monkey in the cradle?" she said.

"For goodness' sake!" said Jane. "She's right!"

"And this bag must have held grandfather's whole supply," said Steve. "The monkey hid it!"

"But how come they didn't find it when they put the cradle away?" Peter demanded.

Kate said, "Well, the monkey died pretty soon. So somebody just put the cradle away. I bet grandfather was looking all over the house for his marbles." She giggled.

"But wait," said Steve. "What about all the marbles we've found all over the house?"

"Why, don't you see!" Peter yelled. "We thought your grandfather lost them. I bet the monkey swiped them from him and put them in all those funny places!"

"And the thread and the thimble!" said Jane.

"And Aunt Matilda's hair bow!" said Kate.

"Of course!" they all shouted.

They were so excited that they jumped up and did a war dance with loud whoops.

Suddenly a window was thrown open. Aunt Matilda put her head out and asked in a worried voice, "Children, what's the matter?"

They all looked up at her. "Oh, nothing!" they shouted. "We're just happy!"

She looked puzzled. "Well, be a *little* quiet," she said, and put the window down.

The four children sat down on the grass again and tried to hold the giggles in. But it was hard. They had made a wonderful discovery.

CHAPTER 13

A Search in
the Sycamore

After a while they calmed down. They had made a discovery, all right, but they had to figure out what it meant.

"If the monkey hid all those marbles and the other things," said Peter, "how come nobody ever found them until now?"

"I don't know," Steve said, shaking his head. "I just never thought of feeling on that ledge over the windows. I've been up there plenty of times and looked all around and never saw anything. And of course I've been up in the sycamore, but I never thought of looking under those boards until you lost your ball."

"I think I know," said Jane. "If you think a person like yourself has lost something, you look in the places where a person might have put it. You don't think of looking for a marble on top of a window

181

ledge because you know you'd never put it there, unless you were a monkey."

"And of course we're not monkeys," Kate added.

"Maybe that's why they never found the rings," said Peter. "Because maybe the monkey took them."

Steve and Kate and Jane stared at him for a minute in silence. Then they all nodded their heads.

"He's right!" said Steve. "That's the truth. The monkey took them! And we never thought of it!"

Now they had a real discovery on their hands. It changed everything. It gave them so much to think about that they couldn't talk. Suddenly they all began to talk at once.

"But how——!"

"But where——"

"But why didn't——"

"Wait a minute," said Steve. "One at a time."

"What I want to know," said Jane, "is, how did the monkey get the rings? They were in a secret drawer, and your great-grandmother never let anybody come into the room when she opened it."

"Oh, that's easy," said Peter. "He sat in the tree. Don't you remember, you're the one who said somebody might have sat in the sycamore and looked in through the window?"

182

"That's right," said Steve, "and a monkey can imitate. He saw how she opened the drawer, and when she went out of the room——"

"He jumped across to the window," Peter shouted.

"Of course," said Steve. "A monkey could do it."

"And he stole the rings——"

"They were in a little leather bag," said Kate, "just like the marbles. Aunt Matilda said so once."

"And what did he do with them?"

"Why, maybe he jumped right back to the tree!" said Jane.

"Then all we have to do is dig in the tree," Steve cried. "Come on!" He jumped up and started climbing the tree. Peter and the girls hurried after him.

"Hey, wait a minute," said Steve. "There isn't room for so many up there."

"Well, it isn't fair for you to have all the fun," Jane complained.

"I tell you what let's do," Peter suggested. "Instead of throwing the sawdust and stuff overboard, couldn't we rig up a bucket with a rope? Then we could let the bucket down and dump it in a pile and we'd be sure not to lose anything."

"Okay." Steve ran for a bucket and rope. The rope was hung over a limb of the tree with the bucket on one end, and the girls held on to the other end.

Peter and Steve climbed up and began to dig out sawdust. They filled the bucket and the girls let it down and began to sift through it while the boys filled the bucket again. They went deeper and deeper into the tree, but no little leather bag appeared. Nothing but acorns and sawdust.

But suddenly there was a shout from the girls.

"Look! Look!" they cried.

Peter peered over the edge. The Lieutenant had stopped looking for the mouse and had come to see what the children were doing. Now he was digging furiously at the foot of the sycamore. The dirt flew out between his hind legs as his forelegs worked.

"He's getting right into the tree!" said Kate. "Come on down and look!"

The boys climbed down and watched. A shower of acorns and sawdust flew out.

"Hey, I think this tree is hollow all the way down!" said Steve.

"Let's poke in from the bottom and see what happens," said Peter.

Kate ran for a stick and Steve poked.

"It feels all soft in there," he said. And suddenly

184

The Lieutenant was digging furiously under the sycamore

there was a rattle and a crash, and a cloud of dust rose up out of the hollow.

"Ka-choo!" the boys sneezed.

"It all fell down," said Steve. "Come on. Now we dig it out at the bottom."

They climbed down and Steve got shovels. There was a small hole at the foot of the tree. They scooped the dust out through this until there was a pile of it on the grass behind them, and Steve, peering up, could see daylight through the trunk of the tree.

"That's all," he said.

But where were the rings? They stared at the pile of dust as though they expected to see a little leather bag suddenly appear.

"I guess," said Steve, "that they aren't there."

"No," said Peter. "I guess not."

He was terribly disappointed.

"We could go through that stuff again," Jane suggested half-heartedly. "Maybe we missed them."

"Okay," said Steve. "Tomorrow. I guess we have to stop now. It's five o'clock."

"Yes. We have to go," said Jane. "May I take my doll home to show Mother?"

186

Kate nodded. She brought one of the blankets from the cradle and wrapped up the doll's clothes for Jane to carry, and then she took another one and laid it over the pile of dust.

"That'll keep it from blowing away till we look through it again," she said.

"Sure," said Steve. But they all knew it was no use.

CHAPTER 14

A Gift for Peter

The next day they got a rake and looked through the dust-pile again, but there was nothing there. They hadn't expected to find anything. Steve shoveled it all into a wheelbarrow and dumped it behind the chicken house.

"Now what shall we do?" Peter asked.

"After wasting all that time," Jane added.

But Steve pointed out that the time hadn't been wasted. They had to look everywhere, and now they had finished with the sycamore.

"I tell you what," said Peter, "we'll just have to look in every place where a monkey could hide something."

Aunt Matilda was still busy in the attic. She didn't really need them, so they spent the whole afternoon climbing up and getting grimy, feeling on top of moldings and behind picture frames.

"Gosh, I'm glad I'm not a monkey," said Jane. "It would be awful to spend your whole life climbing around the walls."

"Maybe they're under a rug somewhere," Peter said. "That would be a change from the ceilings."

But Kate didn't think so. After all, the floors had been swept quite a few times in the last sixty years, and a little leather bag would have been found.

They went out to the back step to think.

"Let's try to get the monkey's point of view," said Peter. "What was going on while he was in the tree watching your great-grandmother?"

"Well, let's see," said Steve. "They were getting ready for the artist. Aunt Matilda and grandfather were in the parlor all dressed up, and their mother told them to stay there till she went up and got the little box. While she was gone, maybe grandfather had to catch the monkey, so he called him, and the monkey came in from outdoors——"

"With the bag in his hand?" Jane asked.

"No," said Steve. "That's no good."

"Well, let's figure it out another way," said Peter. "Maybe the monkey had been up to the bedroom already, and came down to the parlor and hid the bag somewhere in the parlor when nobody was

looking. And then when their mother went up she
couldn't find the rings——"

"And when she came down they were all waiting
for her in the parlor," said Jane. "Well, suppose we
look in the parlor, then."

"All right," said Steve. "We've looked everywhere except there and in the attic."

"I don't think they would be in the attic," said
Kate. "They probably always kept the attic door
closed, the way we do now——"

"Unless they're in something that used to be down here and then got taken up to the attic," said Jane. "Like the marbles in the cradle."

"Well, we can't hunt there while Aunt Matilda's there," said Steve. "So let's try the parlor."

Hunting in the parlor was not easy. They had to be very careful not to knock anything over, and the parlor was full of breakable things that could easily be knocked over. There were vases and boxes and jars. There were lots of little tables with drawers in them. There was the glass cabinet, with all the little carved animals inside, and on the bottom shelf, the little black lacquer box itself in which the jewels had once been kept.

They couldn't look inside the cabinet, because it

was locked. But it was easy to see everything inside it, and there certainly was nothing that looked like a little bag with two rings inside. Steve brought the kitchen stool and climbed up to look on the top of the cabinet but there was nothing but a lot of dust.

At last they had to give it up. They sat down wearily on the sofa and dusted their dirty hands.

"I guess it's not in here," said Steve.

"Unless it's in the chandelier," said Jane, looking up at the crystals hanging from the ceiling.

"Well, if it's in there we'll need a tall ladder to get it," said Steve.

"I want to look at the picture again," Jane said.

So Steve got up and pulled the cord. The red velvet curtains swung aside and there were the boy and the girl looking out at them, and the monkey perched on the boy's shoulder. There was a mischievous look on his little brown face.

Peter stepped close to the picture and peered at it.

"What did you do with those rings?" he demanded. But the monkey wouldn't tell.

Peter sighed. He put up his hand and stroked the smooth brown hull of the *Flying Swallow* that stood on the mantel in front of the picture.

Then Steve pulled the cord and covered the pic-

Peter stepped close to the painting and peered at it

ture, and they all went out into the hall.

They met Aunt Matilda coming down the stairs.

By good luck she didn't appear to notice how dirty they were. She was too busy with her plans.

"I have decided, children," she said, "that in about a week we will have a sale. Mrs. Bowman has convinced me that many people would like to buy things we have, and I know some of them are quite valuable. So we must have a real house cleaning."

Steve looked very unhappy. "Why must we clean house?" he asked. "What difference does it make if people are going to take the things away anyhow?"

"The people will come here and go through the house," said Aunt Matilda. "And we couldn't let them see it dirty."

She went on into the kitchen.

Steve sat down on the stairs and scowled. "House cleaning is bad enough for ourselves," he muttered, "but when it's just for a lot of people to walk through the house and take things away——"

"Look," Jane said, "don't be angry. This will give us a good chance to look some more. We'll all help."

"Well, that's true," said Steve, brightening up a little. "Okay. Operation House Cleaning, we'll call it."

194

But Peter wasn't listening. Suddenly he knew what he wanted Aunt Matilda to give him, the one thing he couldn't bear to think of anybody else taking away. The *Flying Swallow*.

"Steve," he said, "would you mind a lot if I asked your aunt to give me the ship model—you know, the one in there on the mantel?"

He felt he had no right to ask for it. It was Steve's. But Steve didn't mind.

"Of course," he said. "Go ahead. I don't care."

"Are you sure?" Peter asked.

"Yes, I'm sure," said Steve. "I told you I wanted the rooster. If I can't have the real chickens and the goat and the garden I don't especially want anything, but I'll take the stuffed rooster along to remind me. And then some day I'll have a real farm of my own. You'll see."

So Peter followed Aunt Matilda into the kitchen and asked her about the *Flying Swallow*.

She smiled at him. "Yes," she said, putting her hand on his shoulder. "I'd like you to have it. You really appreciate it, and it ought to be yours. I think my father would have liked you to have it."

"I wish I could have seen the real one," said Peter. "I wish I could have gone up in the cupola and seen her coming into the harbor."

"Yes," said Aunt Matilda. "I wish you could. It was the most beautiful sight in the world. Come, I'll give you the ship now."

And she went to the parlor and lifted the little ship down from the mantel and put it into Peter's hands.

"I'll be very careful with it," he said.

"I know you will," said Aunt Matilda.

CHAPTER 15

The *Flying Swallow*

Carefully Peter carried the little ship home. He could hardly believe that it was really his. It was the most wonderful thing he had ever had. He walked so slowly that Jane got tired of waiting for him.

"Hurry up!" she urged.

"I don't want to trip," he explained. "If I fell down I'd smash this ship. You go on ahead."

Jane ran on and Peter, glad to be alone, sat down on the curb and held the *Flying Swallow* in his lap. For a while he just sat there and looked at it.

At last he got up and went home. Jane held the door open for him.

"Well, it certainly took you long enough," she said. "Come on, help me set the table. There's a letter from Dad, and Mother won't read it to us till after supper."

Peter set the *Flying Swallow* carefully on his work bench and came out to help Jane in the kitchen, while Mother put the twins to bed. He didn't really care whether he had supper or not this evening, but he supposed he would have to be polite and join his family.

After supper Mother read them Dad's letter. It was a good letter, full of interesting remarks about the voyage. Dad's ship was in Rio, and he was taking a trip inland while they waited for cargo. He had seen a native village in the jungle, and was bringing them presents. And the best news of all was that he would be home in three weeks!

At any other time this would have been occasion for a grand celebration, but now it fell flat. In three weeks Sea View might be emptied of all its beautiful things. It might even be sold and the Jessups might be gone. Dad wouldn't be able to see it.

Peter got away as soon as he could and went back to his room. He sat down at his work bench and looked at the *Flying Swallow*. Well, Dad would be able to see this anyhow.

He touched the little masts and spars. Lovingly he fingered the sails and the tiny lifeboats. He examined the ropes to see how they were fastened. He

ran his fingernail under the hatch cover to see if it would come off.

It was a little loose. Gently he pried all around it. It seemed to be stuck, but it had been made to come off, for it moved when he ran his nail around the edge. He wondered whether Great-grandfather Jessup had put any cargo in the hold.

Peter put the end of his screwdriver under the edge and pried. Suddenly, with a little wooden squeak, the hatch cover flew off.

199

There *was* something in the hold. It felt like old stiff leather. He put his fingers in and pulled and out came a tiny leather bag. There was something in it. Trembling with excitement, he pulled the bag open. There in his hand lay two rings! One had a red stone, the other a green one.

He sat there staring at them. They sparkled in his hand like—like jewels, he thought. This was what people meant when they said something sparkled like jewels!

Then suddenly he began to shout: "Mom! Jane! Come here, quick! Hurry up!"

There was a sound of running footsteps and his mother and Jane burst in.

"What's the matter? What are you yelling about? You'll wake the babies!" his mother exclaimed. And then she saw what he had in his hand.

Jane saw it too and shrieked. "You *found* them!"

"What's the meaning of this?" his mother asked. "You found what? Where did you get those rings?"

"They were in the hold!" Peter shouted. "Yippee!" And clutching the rings in his fist he jumped up and pranced around the room, and Jane danced with him.

"Peter!" Mother said severely. "Jane! Stop

that. Stop that shouting at once and tell me what this is all about."

They calmed down then and Peter explained how they had been looking for the missing rings, and how he had found them in the hold of the *Flying Swallow*.

Mother took the rings and examined them. "They are really beautiful," she said. "They must be very valuable."

"Oh, they are!" Peter assured her. "Aunt Matilda's father had to sell his ship because he couldn't find them."

"They look like traffic lights," said Jane. "Red and green."

"Port and starboard," Peter corrected her. "They're the ship's running lights. We better take them back to Sea View so they won't run aground in the fog."

Mother laughed. "That's a nice thought," she said. "I'll put them away and we'll take them back in the morning."

But Peter and Jane wouldn't hear of that. "Oh, Mother, we can't! We have to take them tonight," Peter protested.

"I wouldn't be able to sleep a wink if we didn't,"

Jane assured her.

"But we can't leave the babies," said Mother.

That made Peter and Jane laugh at her. "You want to go just as much as we do," said Jane.

So Mother went next door and got Mrs. MacDermott to come and sit with the babies for an hour.

Peter put the rings back inside the *Flying Swallow*, and they set out for Sea View.

They had never been there at night before. The big house was dark, except for the light in the kitchen, shining through the honeysuckle vines on

the porch. Bessie growled as they stepped on the gravel, and Aunt Matilda came to the door. They could see her outlined against the kitchen light.

"Who is it?" she called.

"It's us!" Jane shouted. "It's me and Peter and Mother, and we came to bring——"

But here Peter put his hand over her mouth and threatened to sit on her if she didn't keep still, and Mother backed him up.

"Be quiet, dear," she said. "We have to break this gently."

"Well, this is a nice surprise," said Aunt Matilda, as they went in. "We were just sitting in the kitchen, but come, we'll go into the dining room and have some lemonade and cookies——"

"Oh, no," said Mother, taking the *Flying Swallow* from Peter. "We don't want to stay more than a few minutes."

Steve and Kate stood by the table, staring at the ship. They knew something had happened, but they couldn't figure out what.

"I'm afraid, Miss Jessup," said Mother, "that you've given my son a very valuable present. Too valuable by far."

"Oh, no," said Aunt Matilda. "Please don't say that. It's true it's a family piece, but nobody could appreciate it more than Peter, and I want him to have it. Stephen is more interested in things like animals or I should have kept it for him."

"Wait," said Mother, "you don't know what I mean. This little ship is beautifully made."

"I know," said Aunt Matilda. "Everything my father made was perfect."

"It's so perfect," said Mother, "that even these little lids——"

"Hatch covers," Peter interrupted.

"Even these little hatch covers come off. And when Peter took this one off"—and she lifted the cover— "he found something inside. Something very valuable, as I said before."

Steve and Kate gasped and leaned forward to look into the hold, and Aunt Matilda began to have an idea what Mother was talking about. Her face became pale.

"Do you mean—oh, no, it couldn't be!" she whispered.

"Yes, it is," said Mother. "It's something you've been looking for a long, long time." And she pulled out the little leather bag and put it into Aunt Matilda's hand.

Aunt Matilda opened the bag and the two rings glowed in the lamplight.

"My goodness!" she breathed. "My goodness!" Then she couldn't say anything more for a while. She wiped her eyes and sat looking at the rings.

"It's amazing," Mother said. "To think that they've been there all this time! And it's so wonderful that they're found. I can see that they're very valuable."

"Yes, they are," said Aunt Matilda. "My mother's rings!" She seemed dizzy with surprise.

205

"It seems," said Mother, "that the children have been searching for them for quite a while. They were sure the rings were here somewhere."

"Oh, they were!" said Aunt Matilda. "Well! That explains all the mysterious noises I've been hearing." She laughed, and then the children laughed too.

"We thought we were being very quiet," said Steve.

"Oh, did you?" said Aunt Matilda. "With all those thumps and bumps? But what made you think they were in the house? We decided long ago that they had been stolen."

"We figured out that the monkey must have taken them," said Steve. "Only we couldn't find where he had put them."

"The monkey!" said Aunt Matilda. "Well, we never thought of that! How did you figure it out?"

"We kept finding little things," said Peter. "Marbles and a spool of thread and your hair bow. And we thought the thief must have watched from the sycamore to see how the secret drawer opened."

"Only nobody but a monkey could have jumped across," said Steve. "And then we found the marbles in the cradle——"

"And the marble in the secret drawer," said Aunt Matilda. "The monkey put it there after he took the rings out. It explains everything—so many little things kept disappearing. And we thought Thomas always lost his marbles! And now I remember——"

"What, Aunt Matilda?" Steve asked.

"That monkey was always so fond of sitting on the mantel shelf. But he never seemed to be doing any harm there. He never knocked anything down. So we let him sit there."

She felt in the hold of the ship.

"Is there anything else in there?" Steve asked.

Aunt Matilda pulled out a silk handkerchief. It was very thin and old and yellow.

"The little rascal!" she said. "He had it packed very neatly. That's why it never rattled."

And then she seemed to forget all of the others and just sat and looked at the rings in her hand.

Mother stood up. "We must go back," she said. "Mrs. MacDermott is staying with the twins. Come, Peter and Jane."

Peter and Jane would rather have stayed. But they followed Mother to the door.

Just as they got there, however, Aunt Matilda said, "Oh, but Peter must take the ship."

207

"Oh, no," said Mother. "Now you'll be staying here, and the ship belongs here."

"If it weren't for these children," said Aunt Matilda, "we wouldn't be here. The ship belongs to Peter. I don't know how to thank you———"

"Don't try," said Mother. "Good night. We'll see you tomorrow." And she steered Peter and Jane out through the door.

CHAPTER 16

Aunt Matilda Goes to Town

Well, of course, the next morning nothing could keep Peter and Jane at home, and so, as they still had the twins to mind, they put them into their carriage and wheeled them to Sea View as fast as they could.

Steve and Kate ran out to meet them. Kate flung her arms around Jane, and gave her a big kiss, and was as noisy as Jane herself, and even the serious Steve leaped around and yelled, "Yippee!"

The babies looked up at him and laughed as though he were doing it for their benefit. The Lieutenant got excited and raced around barking wildly.

"We're going to stay!" Steve yelled. "Hooray! Hooray! We're going to stay!"

Aunt Matilda had called up her lawyer and told him about the rings. She was going to town that very day to have them appraised by a jeweler,

209

which meant to find out how much they were worth. They had decided to sell Taffy but they thought they would be able to keep the chickens—at least some of them—and they were going to have new pipes put in, and the roof fixed! And all the time they were doing the Indian war dance.

But Peter had something else on his mind.

"You know," he said, "there's still a matter of business to be attended to. We haven't finished Operation Stove. What about the money we earned?"

"That's right," said Steve. "I'd forgotten all about that. What'll we do?"

"Well," said Peter, "I suggest we buy the stove anyway. Because even if your aunt does have new plumbing put in, she might still have to keep that old stove, and even if she decided to buy a new stove, it might not be for a long time."

"Okay," said Steve. "Let's go this afternoon. She's going to town, so it's perfect."

Steve had not done his chores yet, so the girls took the babies out on the lawn, and Steve and Peter went to feed the animals.

Abigail strutted up and down the chicken yard, clucking to her chicks, which were all growing nicely and beginning to get feathers. Abigail's black feathers shone in the sun.

Steve looked at her proudly. "I bet that hen would take a prize at a fair," he said. "By golly, the next time there's a fair I'm going to exhibit her." He tossed a measure of corn out on the ground.

"You know," he said, "yesterday I didn't want to look at those chicks. But now I know we're going to stay—yippee!" And he yelled so loudly that Abigail gathered her children quickly under her wings.

"Don't worry," said Steve. "I won't hurt them. Come on, Pete, we'd better get outside where I can yell if I want to."

In the afternoon the four children set out for Mr. Bunch's store.

"We've come for our stove," Steve told Mr. Bunch.

"Well, now, that's fine," said Mr. Bunch. "I'm still holding it for you. It's right there in the back."

"We thought for a while," Steve explained, "that we wouldn't be able to get it, because Aunt Matilda was going to have to sell the house. But now we're pretty sure she isn't. So we want to get it this afternoon while she's in town."

A broad smile spread over Mr. Bunch's face. "Well, now," he said, "if that isn't the best news I've heard in ages. I did hear she might have to sell, and I would hate to see Matilda Jessup leave."

"We would have hated it too," said Steve.

"I know you would, boy," said Mr. Bunch. "And I'd hate to see that old house come down. I heard that Mr. Krautkopf was going to put up a supermarket. Nothing wrong with a supermarket, but why should he put it where your house is? There's lots of empty land. Just wants to own everything, that's what!"

Mr. Bunch said he was just setting out to make some deliveries, so he loaded the stove on his truck and left his assistant in charge, and they drove back to Sea View. They hoisted the stove down from the truck and into the kitchen, and put it in front of the windows, and then Steve ran out and got two pots of geraniums and stood them on the stove. The red flowers looked very nice with the white enamel of the stove.

Then they printed a sign saying:

To Aunt Matilda, so you won't get too hot cooking on the big stove. From the four of us and Mr Bunch. XXXXX

Mr. Bunch objected to the five X's that Jane put at the bottom. He said an X stood for a kiss and he didn't want Matilda Jessup to misunderstand, but Kate said she wouldn't. She would just know that the stove was partly from him.

Mr. Bunch patted her cheek and said he was glad to help any time, and then he went out and got in his truck and drove away.

Aunt Matilda stopped suddenly in front of the stove

All this had taken a good deal of time, and when Aunt Matilda came home they were sitting on the top step of the porch, watching for her. They expected to see her walking along the street, but they didn't. Suddenly a taxi appeared. It came right up the driveway and stopped, and Aunt Matilda got out. Her face was red and her hat was on crooked, and she called to the children and then dived back into the taxi. The driver got out and began pulling packages out. The whole taxi was full of bundles.

"Aunt Matilda!" said Steve, looking very worried. "What's in all these bundles?" He seemed to think his aunt was not quite in her right mind. She had never behaved like this before.

"You shall see, Stephen," she said. "Be patient."

They all helped to carry the things up on the porch and Aunt Matilda paid the driver and sent him away, though he was quite anxious to stay and find out what was going on.

Then Aunt Matilda said, "Now I'll just go into the kitchen and get a drink of water, and then you shall see what I brought." She hurried into the kitchen, and then she stopped suddenly.

"Oh!" she said, and her voice sounded squeaky, as if it didn't belong to her. "Children! Come here!"

She turned to look for them. They were crowding into the doorway, grinning at her.

"Surprise!" they shouted, and then they ran and hugged her.

"It's beautiful!" Aunt Matilda exclaimed. "It's just beautiful!" She bent over to read the sign and a drop splashed on the white enamel. She felt in her pocket for a handkerchief and sat down, as if she were too weak to stand up any more. "Just imagine you children buying me a stove! How on earth did you earn the money?"

"Minding babies, mostly," said Jane.

"That's why we let the ladies pay us," Steve explained. "We really needed the money. We didn't think you'd mind."

Aunt Matilda shook her head. "No," she said. "I don't really mind. I think you children are very smart. Now I must just get my breath. I haven't had a day like this in I don't know when!"

After she was rested, she had to try the stove, and it was wonderful. She loved it. It was just what she wanted and she didn't know why she hadn't bought one long ago.

"I guess we couldn't afford it, Aunt Matilda," Steve reminded her.

But she shook her head. "It wasn't only that," she said. "It was partly that I've always wanted things to be just the way they always were. But it's going to be different now."

"Why, Aunt Matilda?" Kate asked.

"Well," she said, "I think it's this. When I thought I really would have to sell the house, I made myself get used to the idea of having *everything* different. But now that we're going to stay, it won't be hard to have some of the things different. In fact, it's going to be *fun!*"

Then she remembered the packages.

"You children bring them in here," she said, "and get some scissors, and I'll show you what's in them."

She began cutting strings and tearing off paper, and as she worked she told how she had gone to the jeweler, and had found out that the rings were even more valuable than she had thought, much more valuable than they had been sixty years ago. The jeweler had bought them from her. She had put most of the money in the bank, but saved some to go shopping with. There was a present for each child.

There was a book of ship pictures for Peter, and a camera for Steve so that he could take pictures of his goat and chickens and keep a record of them. There were some mystery books for Jane, and for Kate a baby doll in a basket.

But the other packages were full of very surprising things. There were blocks and drawing paper and balls and toy trains!

"Aunt Matilda!" said Steve, looking worried again. "What is all this stuff for?"

And then Aunt Matilda sprang the real surprise. "I'm going to have a nursery school!" she said. "I just knew there must be a *good* reason why Sea

View should be preserved, not a selfish one, and it has come to me. There's no park here. Those babies need a shady lawn to play on and I have it. I love the babies, and you children are getting so grown up that soon you won't need to be taken care of at all. So the mothers may bring the children here and I'll take care of them. I'll—I'll go into business!"

Kate's eyes opened wide and she smiled.

"Oh, Aunt Matilda, that's wonderful!" she said. "And I'll help you!" And she put her arms around her great-aunt's neck and gave her a hug that nearly choked her.

"Of course you will," said Aunt Matilda.

"But Aunt Matilda," said Jane. "You mean you're going to let the mothers pay to bring the children here?"

"Of course, child," said Aunt Matilda, her eyes twinkling. "I know I scolded you for doing the same thing. But I've been thinking since then that you children had more sense than I had. Here we have a big house, and it's the only thing we do have to make a living with, only it had to be fixed up a bit. Now we have the money to fix it up, though not enough to live on the rest of our lives. So it's only sensible to go on where you children started. And now," she added briskly, "we'll have supper. I must use that new stove."

"Aren't you tired?" Steve asked.

"Tired!" said Aunt Matilda. "Not a bit. Kate, you just get up off my lap and I'll show you whether I'm tired. And Peter and Jane, you must stay for supper. Run home and tell your mother. Goodness! Tell your mother to come too."

"But the twins!" Jane reminded her.

"Oh, my. Well, tell her to bring the twins too. They can go to sleep in their carriage. It won't hurt them. Hurry now."

Peter didn't think Mother would come, but she did. She just couldn't wait to hear about Aunt Matilda's trip to town. They put the surprised twins into their carriage and hitched up the Lieutenant and hurried over to Sea View. Aunt Matilda had supper almost ready by the time they arrived, and it was so cool with the new stove that they were able to eat supper in the kitchen.

All through supper Mother and Aunt Matilda talked about the nursery school. Mother was going to help get it organized. She was just as excited as Aunt Matilda.

After supper the girls washed the dishes and

Mother took the twins out on the porch and put them to sleep in their carriage. Aunt Matilda sat in her rocking chair and rested.

Peter and Steve were looking at Peter's new book at the kitchen table.

Into the middle of this peaceful scene came the blast of a horn. A small green car had stopped at the end of the driveway and a short stout man had gotten out.

Aunt Matilda got up. "It's Mr. Krautkopf."

Mr. Krautkopf came stamping up the walk.

"Good evening, Miss Jessup!" he shouted. He seemed angry.

"Sh!" said Aunt Matilda. "Please, not so loud. You'll wake the babies."

"I don't know anything about babies," said Mr. Krautkopf. "I have just heard in a very roundabout way——"

Aunt Matilda stood at the top of the steps with her hands on her hips. "I will write you a letter, Mr. Krautkopf," she said.

"I don't care about a letter," said Mr. Krautkopf. "You have practically made an agreement with me."

"I am not selling the house, if that's what you mean," said Aunt Matilda.

Mr. Krautkopf stopped and looked up angrily at Aunt Matilda. Aunt Matilda looked calmly down at him. "Good night, Mr. Krautkopf," she said.

Mr. Krautkopf turned around and stamped back to his car. With an angry scraping of gears he drove away.

Aunt Matilda sighed. "He is such a difficult man to get along with," she said. "I always want to be polite to him, but I just can't."

"I don't want to be polite to him," said Steve.

"I'm sorry he is angry," said Aunt Matilda gently. "I should like everybody to be happy tonight."

She rocked in her chair. The children had come out and sat on the top step. Mother pushed the carriage quietly back and forth.

The night air was warm and sweet with the smell of honeysuckle, and fireflies danced under the trees like little lamps. In the dark trees the locusts shrilled. Somewhere a cricket chirped.

The Lieutenant came and crawled into Peter's lap, and went to sleep there.

"It's almost September," said Jane.

"Pretty soon Dad will be home," said Peter. "And Sea View will still be here for him to see."

CHAPTER 17

Dad Comes Home

For the next few weeks Sea View was there, all right, but it didn't look the same at all.

Workmen came and brought ladders and tools and machinery. They dug trenches for the pipes. They broke holes in the walls. They made a great noise and a still greater mess.

Poor old Bessie had never heard anything like it. She barked until she was hoarse and Aunt Matilda had to shut her up in the cellar. The Lieutenant got so excited that he had to be left at home. The chickens got excited too, and squawked and clucked all the time. But Taffy the goat was gone.

Taffy had been a problem. Steve and Aunt Matilda had decided that she ought to be sold or sent away, but where could they send her? Aunt Matilda found out about a farm far away where they kept goats, yet Steve was worried. How would he know they would be kind to Taffy?

And then they remembered Mr. Bunch. He had said he would be glad to help if he could. Steve went to see him. And Mr. Bunch said yes, he knew of a farm only twenty miles away that might take her. So Mother drove Taffy and the children to the farm one day, and they were glad to see her safely settled in a big field with six other goats. The farmer said Steve could come and see her whenever he liked.

Mr. Bunch was a help in other ways too. It seemed that Aunt Matilda was not merely going to have new pipes. No, indeed. She was going to have a wonderful kitchen just like Mother's, with a dish-washer and a washing machine and a fine big refrigerator.

So Mr. Bunch was helping her plan what to buy, and about half the time his truck was parked outside at the back driveway, and he was walking around, mopping his forehead with his handkerchief, and advising Aunt Matilda, while Aunt Matilda listened respectfully and made notes on a pad.

"Now you see," he would say, "you can put the sink by the window, and the dish-washer next to it, and the refrigerator on the left, and then the electric stove on the right——"

But on the subject of stoves Aunt Matilda was firm. She was going to have an electric dish-washer and refrigerator, but the stove, she insisted, was going to be the one the children had bought her.

"Now, Miss Jessup," said Mr. Bunch, "that's a nice stove. I helped picked it out myself, and I think you ought to keep it in case there's an electric storm and the current is off. But you really ought to have one of these new stoves——"

"No, Mr. Bunch," said Aunt Matilda. "This stove is just fine. It will do for now very nicely, and the old range will be there for winter because it warms up the house. I just wouldn't know what to do without it in winter. And the new one will be fine for summer. Maybe another year I'll get one of those new-fangled electric ones with all the fancy switches on the front, but not now."

And nothing Mr. Bunch could say would dissuade her.

Of course Peter and Jane couldn't be there all the time. With all the confusion and construction going on, the babies had to stay at home, so Peter and Jane rushed over right after breakfast, and then rushed home again to mind the twins, and rushed back after lunch. It was a long hot walk, but what could they do? They couldn't stay away.

One day, as they were starting out after lunch, there was Mr. Bunch's truck pulled up in front of their house.

The Lieutenant rushed out and barked furiously to show what a good watch-dog he was.

"Belay there, Lieutenant!" said Peter. "Hello, Mr. Bunch."

"Ahoy," said Mr. Bunch. "Stand by to take off some cargo."

"Cargo for us?" Peter asked.

"Aye, aye, sir," said Mr. Bunch. He climbed into the back of his truck and handed Peter—a bicycle!

But what a bicycle! It was gleaming with red enamel and nickel plating, and the spokes of the wheels glittered in the sun as they spun round. Peter was too stunned to move. He just stood there holding it and staring at it.

"Now the young lady," said Mr. Bunch, and he handed another one down to Jane—a girl's bike this time, enameled in blue.

"Well, good-by," he said, climbing back into the driver's seat. "I'll see you there." And he drove off.

When Peter and Jane could move, they ran to Mother's study.

"Mother!" they shouted. "Look what Mr. Bunch left! How come? Did you tell him to do it?"

Mother smiled and pointed to the sheet of paper in her typewriter. In the middle of the page, under the last line of typing, was the word FINIS.

"My book is done," she said. "I could never have done it so soon without you two, and since you're running back and forth so much, I decided you ought to have your reward now."

"Oh, Mom!" they cried, and threw themselves on her, nearly knocking her over.

Then they ran out and jumped on their new bikes and pedaled off to Sea View.

It didn't seem far at all. Peter couldn't understand why he had considered it a long walk.

"And it's cool," he shouted, as the breeze blew past his ears. "I feel a lot cooler than I did this morning."

"Me too," Jane shouted back.

Then one day a cable arrived. "Ship docks Thursday two P.M. Dad." It came at lunch time.

"This is Tuesday," said Mother. "We have two days to get the house cleaned up. We must get busy right away."

Then there was a great scrubbing of decks and polishing of portholes. Every bit of brightwork had to be shined up, for the Commander mustn't come home to a dirty ship. The crew had to have haircuts all around and an issue of fresh dungarees, and the Lieutenant had to have a bath and a brushing, which he didn't like a bit.

On Tuesday evening Peter and Jane rode wearily over to Sea View to explain why they hadn't been there earlier.

"Dad's coming home," Peter said. "If only the

ship would dock at Sea Harbor, we wouldn't have to wait so long."

"You know," said Steve, "the ships all go past here, even if they don't dock. If we only knew what time your father's ship would pass, we could be watching."

"We'll call up the company!" said Jane, tossing her dark hair enthusiastically.

So the next day Mother telephoned. She had a hard time making the company understand what she wanted, but at last somebody said he thought the *Mary K. Sterling* might go past Sea Harbor between nine and ten in the morning.

On Thursday morning at eight o'clock the four children were up in the cupola. Peter had his mother's opera glasses and Steve brought up his great-grandfather's telescope, and they took turns watching, fifteen minutes apiece.

For a long time there was nothing to be seen but

230

some fishing boats and a few catboats. But at last Peter, sweeping the horizon with his spyglass, called out, "Steamer sighted on the starboard bow!"

"Let me see!" Jane cried, reaching for the glasses.

Peter gave them to her. "I see it, I see it!" she said.

Far off, a tiny dot crept across the ocean. Through the glasses they could see two blue stripes and one red stripe on the funnels.

"That's Dad! He's coming home!" said Peter.

They watched until the ship had crept clear

across the horizon, leaving its trail of smoke behind.

Then Steve closed the windows and they went downstairs.

"If it had been your great-grandfather," said Jane, "we'd know that he would be home in a couple of hours. But Dad probably won't get here until tonight. Oh, dear! Now that we've practically seen him, how will we wait till he gets here?"

They pedaled home. Somehow they had to live through the day. Never had a day crept so slowly.

At last it was two o'clock.

"Now the ship is docking," Jane said.

But they still had to wait for Dad to get off the ship and catch a train. It would take hours more.

They wandered about the house, got up, sat

down—there was nothing they wanted to do. At last Mother sent them off to the store for some ice cream to put in the freezer for supper.

They rode to the store, circling several blocks in order to take longer, and when they came back at last a yellow taxi was just pulling away from the curb. A man was standing on the sidewalk surrounded by suitcases.

They threw themselves off their bikes and screamed, "Daddy! We didn't see you come!"

Mother ran out of the house. The Lieutenant began to bark. The twins began to yell. The neighbors looked out of the windows to see what the excitement was about.

At last Dad managed to disentangle himself from his family.

"I couldn't wait for a train," he said, "and I had all this luggage. So I took a taxi from the city."

They helped him get the things inside. On the way he had to stop to admire the garden, the house, the cleanliness of everything.

The twins had learned to say "Da-da" and "bow-wow."

The Lieutenant was almost grown up.

Jane and Peter were brown, and at least an inch taller.

They all sat down on the sofa. Everybody tried to get nearest to Dad.

Everybody, that is, but the Lieutenant. He was acting very strangely. The hair on his back was sticking up, and he was growling and walking round and round a little wicker basket.

"What's the matter with him?" Peter asked.

Dad laughed. "He's discovered one of the presents," he said. And he got up and picked up the basket.

It moved a bit as he held it on his lap. He took off the lid, and there, crouched in the bottom, with its tiny hands over its face, was a little brown monkey!

Everybody tried to sit on the sofa next to Dad

"A monkey!" Jane and Peter exclaimed, both together. "Oh, Dad, you've brought us a monkey!"

Dad lifted the little creature out and it clung to him with both arms around his neck.

"He's scared now," said Dad. "He's had a long trip. You must let him get used to his new home. Peter, you pat the puppy so he won't be too jealous. They'll get used to each other. And Jane, get a little cup of milk for him. And maybe a piece of banana."

Jane got some milk in one of her doll's cups, and they watched while the monkey drank, holding the cup tightly in his tiny hands. Then he took the banana she offered him. He nibbled a piece, and looked brightly at all the faces around him, and then nibbled some more.

"He's darling," said Jane. "Just wait till Aunt Matilda and Steve and Kate see him!"

"Only be sure that nobody leaves any valuable jewelry around," said Dad, laughing.

"Oh, you got our last letter!" said Mother. "We weren't sure you would. You know how Peter found the rings."

Peter went to his room and came back with the *Flying Swallow*.

236

"This is where they were," he said, opening the hatch. He handed the ship carefully to his father.

Dad examined the little ship. "It's a very exciting story," he said. "You children really were a benefit to the community, weren't you? I can't wait to go to Sea View and meet your friends."

"We'll go after supper," said Mother. "Right now we'll just sit and talk."

"All right," said Dad. He handed the monkey to Jane. It sat on her shoulder and examined the handkerchief in her shirt pocket. Then it pulled it out and wiped its face.

Dad laughed. "He's imitating me. I used to do that in my cabin because it was so hot. He'll copy anything."

"Oh, boy, it's going to be exciting around here from now on," said Peter.

"From now on!" Dad exclaimed. "I think you've had enough excitement already to last you a long time. And that reminds me of something Jane said just before we moved to Sea View Gardens."

"What was it, Dad?" Jane asked.

"You said, as I remember, that nothing exciting could ever happen in a little house like this. That you could never discover a treasure in it."

"Did I really say that?" Jane asked. "I can hardly believe it."

"Yes, you did," said Peter. "And I remember now what Dad answered. He said, 'Don't be too sure.' And he was right. We did discover a treasure, and it was right here in this house!"